A PAST TO FORGET

CONVENIENT ARRANGEMENTS(BOOK 5)

ROSE PEARSON

A PAST TO FORGET

Convenient Arrangements

(Book 5)

By

Rose Pearson

A PAST TO FORGET

PROLOGUE

"You must make a good impression this evening."

Ellen closed her eyes and took in a long, steadying breath. This was now the fifth time that her mother had spoken to her, and Ellen was already all too aware of what was expected of her.

"Lord and Lady Guardmouth are highly respected," Lady Coulbourne continued, running a critical eye over Ellen. "You must behave with all propriety, speaking well and showing both grace and elegance."

"Yes, Mama," Ellen replied, quietly, knowing that she could not say or do anything but agree with Lady Coulbourne. She did not need to remind her mother that this was now her second year in London and that last year, whilst it had not brought her a suitable match, had been quite satisfactory in its own way.

"There will be a good many eligible gentlemen there this evening also," Lady Coulbourne reminded her, her eyes glittering suddenly. "But there is no particular need for you to speak to anyone, although should someone show you interest, then that would be most satisfactory."

This remark puzzled Ellen somewhat, for she surely ought to be doing her level best to make an excellent impression on these unmarried gentlemen. After all, the only reason she was in London was to find a suitable match. Knowing full well that she was not the most beautiful of young ladies, nor the most eligible. Being the daughter of a viscount with a respectable dowry might not be enough to capture the attention of London gentlemen, for they could easily turn their interest to a lady of higher title, with a greater dowry and rather more beauty about her. But surely it was to her advantage to try her best to engage with such gentlemen rather than simply make no effort whatsoever.

"You are frowning, Ellen." Her mother's tone was a little irritated. "There is a line forming between your brows, and it shall remain there permanently if you do not remove it."

Ellen hastily rearranged her features into a less puzzled expression, although she continued to consider what it was her mother had said and what she had meant by such remarks.

"Very well," Lady Coulbourne said eventually, a small sigh escaping her as she shook her head. "I think you will do, Ellen. It seems as though your new lady's maid is satisfactory, after all." She gave Ellen a glimmer of a smile, but it did not comfort Ellen in the least. "Come now, the carriage is waiting."

"Is Father not to attend with us tonight?" Ellen asked,

frowning again and instantly forcing the expression from her face. "I thought he was to join us at the soiree."

Her mother turned back to face her and, instantly, Ellen saw the flicker in her mother's eyes. Her stomach began to tighten as she held Lady Coulbourne's gaze, her chin lifting just a little as she folded her arms in front of her. Her mother knew very well that Ellen could be quite stubborn when she wished it, for she very often chided Ellen for her lack of docility—but on this occasion, Ellen felt justified in her persistence. Something was happening that she was not aware of, and from the expression on her mother's face, Ellen was confident that the matter involved herself in some way or another.

"Your father is gone out," Lady Coulbourne answered, her voice a little higher pitched than before. "He has another, more pressing engagement."

"Mama," Ellen replied, her tone firm and steady. "Where is Father going? What is it that he must speak about that is so important that he must miss Lord Guardmouth's soiree?" She tilted her head just a little. "He already wrote to give his acceptance, did he not? Why now would he change his mind? Surely such behavior could be considered...rather rude?" A challenge in her voice, she fixed her eyes upon her mother and did not even allow herself to blink, seeing the way her mother sighed heavily and looked away, which added all the more to Ellen's distress. She hid such feelings easily, however, making quite certain to simply look purposefully at her mother and press down her own feelings of anxiety and worry. Lady Coulbourne was not someone who could easily hide her emotions, and certainly, Ellen knew, would soon give up whatever it was that she held so tightly to her chest simply because she could not bear the burden of carrying it any longer.

"You are being very foolish indeed, Ellen," Lady Coulbourne stated, placing her hands on her hips and looking back at Ellen with obvious frustration. "Why must you ask such questions? We will be late for the soiree and—"

"Mama," Ellen interrupted, feeling an edge of anger begin to dig into her heart. "You are behaving very strangely, indeed. First of all, you state that there is no particular importance as to whether or not I am greeted by any eligible gentlemen this evening, only then to tell me that father is not attending with us any longer. I cannot imagine what is of such importance that he must simply leave our side in order to go elsewhere!" She shrugged indelicately. "We will not be late for the soiree, Mama, so long as you tell me of whatever it is that is so obviously being hidden from me."

Lady Coulbourne set her jaw, but it did not take long before she relented. Evidently, the idea of being tardy to Lord Guardmouth's soiree was more than she could bear.

"Must you be so stubborn, Ellen?" she sighed, throwing up her hands. "Very well, if you must know the truth, it is that your father is gone to meet with one partic-ular gentleman."

"And for what reason is that?" Ellen demanded, her heart beating furiously as she began to realize precisely what it was that her mother meant by such a statement.

Lady Coulbourne sighed heavily again. "To see if he cannot make an arrangement with him," she said, gesturing towards Ellen. "An arrangement that would suit both families very well."

Her heart began to clamor within her and she looked directly at her mother, knowing what was now before her. "You mean to say that I am to be married off?"

"It is not as bad as all that," Lady Coulbourne said with a dismissive wave of her hand. "Many marriages are arranged, as you well know."

"But I would have thought my father would have had the courtesy to inform me of such a thing *before* he made any sort of arrangement with anyone," Ellen replied, hot tears beginning to burn in her eyes. "Surely, I am old enough to be *told* that such a thing will take place rather than merely being introduced to a gentleman and told that he is to be my husband?"

Lady Coulbourne spread her hands. "Your father does as he thinks is best, my dear," she said without any sign that she agreed with what had been done. "I do as he instructs. You must see that he believes this to be the right course of action to take, for then surely you will be settled and contented, just as your brother is."

"That is very different," Ellen replied tightly, blinking quickly so that tears would not fall to her cheeks. "My brother was given no guidance other than to make certain that his wife was from a good family and had a decent dowry. Thereafter, he was permitted to make his own choice."

"And such is the way with gentlemen," Lady Coulbourne replied sharply. "I will not allow you to start feeling sorry for yourself, Ellen. Your father will have a very suitable gentleman in mind, and I am certain you shall be very happy as his wife."

Ellen closed her eyes and took in a long breath, feeling herself trembling at what had just been revealed to her. She did not feel any sense of contentment but was deeply upset at how her parents had treated her. She felt like a commodity, something that was useful only in the value that could be gained from her sale. To have no knowledge of the gentleman that her father was considering was also frightening, for her father's judgment might be vastly different from her own. What if she was to find herself betrothed to a man only a few years younger than her father? After all, she knew she was not a diamond of the first water, and thus, such an agreement was a much greater possibility.

"*Do* come on, Ellen," her mother said impatiently as her sharp voice interrupted Ellen's tangled thoughts. "You stated you would come with me once I had told you all. I have now done so, and I now expect you to do as you stated."

Ellen wanted to rail at her mother, to ask her how she could do such a thing, how she could leave her in this state of ambivalence when there was something of such great importance going on without her knowledge. Instead, knowing that such a thing was quite futile and would only upset her mother, Ellen forced a breath, set her shoulders, and opened her eyes. Without another word, she made her way past Lady Coulbourne and down the staircase towards the front door.

Her mother was right, the carriage was waiting—but suddenly, the evening's soiree held no interest for Ellen.

It meant nothing. There was no reason for her to attend, other than to see others and to be seen. Her mind would have no rest until she spoke to her father and found out whether or not he had been successful—and just which gentleman, out of the many in London, had been the one her father had chosen. She could only pray that she might find even a modicum of happiness in her future, for without it, Ellen did not know what she would do.

CHAPTER ONE

"And you say this is your daughter's second Season?"

Viscount Coulbourne nodded, picking up his glass and swirling the brandy within it. "Her second, yes." He shrugged. "Last Season, I allowed her to enjoy the months here in London, but now the time has come for her to consider her future seriously."

"And you are doing precisely that, on her behalf," Leonard replied with a small smile. "I am sure she is most grateful."

Lord Coulbourne let out a snort. "She does not know!" he exclaimed with a chuckle. "There is no requirement for her to be aware of such arrangements, given that she is to do precisely what I instruct her to do. No doubt, she will be very glad indeed to know of such a match. That is," he continued, lifting one eyebrow towards Leonard, "if you agree."

Leonard considered things carefully. He had need of a wife, certainly, but he was not yet satisfied with what Lord Coulbourne had said of the lady. He felt as though he knew very little about her, which, for some gentlemen, might be very satisfactory indeed, but it was not enough for him. There was a need within him to know the lady a little better than he did at present, so that he might judge her character and, with it, whether or not she would make him a decent wife. He did not expect them to always have a life of contentment, for marriage was, he believed, a journey that one enjoyed with a suitable companion, but he certainly did not want a harridan for a bride! Lord Coulbourne might have stated that his daughter was a little plain but well taught in all manner of ladylike conduct and interests, but certainly, Leonard was not simply about to take his word for it.

"I should like to meet your daughter before I give my consent," he said as Lord Coulbourne nodded, clearly entirely unconcerned about such a thing. "Should I find her to be as you have described, once I have spent a little more time in her company, then I shall be glad to have her as my bride."

Lord Coulbourne beamed at him and, picking up the last of his brandy, threw it back in one gulp.

"Capital!" he boomed, his loud voice seeming to shake the establishment itself. "When shall we say?"

A little taken aback by Lord Coulbourne's eagerness and wondering if this was simply because he knew that all he had said of his daughter would be quite true, Leonard took a moment to react as Lord Coulbourne hefted himself out of the chair and stuck out his hand. With a little embarrassment, he rose swiftly and shook Lord Coulbourne's hand.

"Shall we say perhaps tomorrow afternoon?" he

suggested, a little surprised that he felt a sense of nervousness creep over him at the realization that he would soon meet the lady who might one day be his wife. "I could call in the afternoon?"

"Capital!" Lord Coulbourne said again, shaking Leonard's hand firmly before mercifully releasing it. "I shall tell Ellen of what is to happen immediately. I can assure you that you will find her very pleasing indeed, Lord Stafford."

"I am sure I shall," Leonard replied quickly, although he told himself, silently, that he would not be chivvied into any sort of arrangement, despite the eagerness of Lord Coulbourne. "Until tomorrow, then."

Lord Coulbourne took his farewell, leaving Leonard standing alone for a few moments. Eventually, he sat down heavily in his chair, his brow furrowed as he considered all that had been said.

Having been introduced to Lord Coulbourne only a short time ago, when the family had returned to London for the Season, Leonard had never once imagined that he would find himself on the verge of being betrothed to Lord Coulbourne's daughter! But when Lord Coulbourne had mentioned, just in passing, that he had to find a suitable husband for his daughter, Leonard had found his interest suddenly piqued.

"You look as though you have something of great distress on your mind rather than what I hope it *should* be."

Leonard pulled himself from his thoughts to look up at his friend, Lord Repington.

"Repington!" he exclaimed, making to get up from his

chair, but his friend gestured for him to sit back down again, before throwing himself into the seat that Lord Coulbourne had only just vacated. "I did not know that you were spying on me."

Viscount Repington chuckled, his eyes half-closed as he studied Leonard with a lazy smile playing about his mouth. "I knew that you were to meet with Lord Coulbourne this evening, and I somehow found my way to Whites also." One brow lifted. "Well? Is all arranged?"

Leonard rolled his eyes. "No, it is not all arranged," he said with a chuckle. "I have not even met the lady as yet!" He laughed again as he saw exasperation fill his friend's face. Lord Repington was his closest acquaintance and had listened to Leonard's woes a good many times. He knew Leonard better than any other soul—possibly even more so than Leonard's own mother—and had been very excited indeed to hear about the possible engagement between Leonard and Lord Coulbourne's daughter.

"I am sure that any daughter of Lord Coulbourne's will be *more* than adequate for you," Lord Repington said with a sigh. "She will be genteel, quite elegant, and always stay within the bounds of propriety. She will be young enough to provide you with as many children as you require and, in addition, shall look very pretty indeed when she walks alongside you."

Leonard smiled and shook his head. "I believe she is a little plain."

"But still, any hint of beauty will do you the world of good," Lord Repington replied with a grin. "It does not matter to you, I should not think, whether or not she is very beautiful."

"You are quite right in that," Leonard agreed. "Given my own appearance, I can have no stipulation when it comes to the lady's beauty."

Lord Repington lifted one eyebrow. "You are allowed to hope that she is attractive, Stafford," he reminded Leonard, suddenly very stoic. "There is nothing wrong in being drawn to one's wife."

"As you would know?" Leonard questioned glibly as Lord Repington chuckled.

"I fear that my difficulty is not that I am not drawn to a potential bride, but that I find too many young ladies to be so lovely and beautiful that I cannot bring myself to choose only one to pursue!" Lord Repington answered with a mocking sigh. "For instance, I was quite persuaded that Lady Josephine would be just the sort of lady I should court, only to find my eye then captured by a very lovely Miss Lawrence, who has the most beautiful blue eyes I have ever seen!"

Leonard shook his head and, catching the attention of the footman, asked for two more brandies. "I think you are to be lost forever," he said with a grin. "Who should have thought that I would be the one to wed before you?"

Lord Repington's smile suddenly faded. "You have a much better character than I, Stafford," he told Leonard, growing quickly serious. "I have always thought that you would wed first, for you are much more a gentleman than I shall ever be!" His brow furrowed, and he dropped his gaze. "I fear that, even if I should marry, I will find myself unable to stay solely by the side of my wife."

A hard kick caught Leonard's stomach, and he forced himself to take a sip of his brandy so that he would not immediately react. There was a deep sense of anger within him over any gentleman who did not remain faithful to his wife, even though it was very common and, indeed, largely accepted for a married gentleman to take a mistress. Leonard now considered that such anger came from the pain of knowing what his mother had been forced to endure for the many, many years she had been wed to Leonard's father. The late Lord Stafford had been nothing more than selfish and had made his own choices without giving even a modicum of consideration to his wife. In fact, Leonard could recall the times that his father had drunk far too much liquor and had then gone on to boast to his son about the many, many ladies he had taken to bed. It had repulsed Leonard, forcing him, in the end, away from his father's estate and towards London, where he had resided until his father had passed away.

Upon return, he had found his mother pale, tired, and worn with grief—but Leonard had been certain it had not been sorrow over her husband's death but over the life she had been forced to endure. Silently, he had determined that he should never become the same sort of gentleman as his father.

"You will think very poorly of me, I believe, should I ever do such a thing," Lord Repington said sadly. "Believe me, it would not be my intention at first, but I fear I am very weak when it comes to such matters."

"Then perhaps you should find a lady whose heart makes you fall so desperately in love with her that you cannot think of any other," he replied as Lord Repington threw his head back and laughed. "You may think me ridiculous, but I have heard of such things occurring!"

Lord Repington shook his head. "I think I should fail even more," he said with a shrug. "Perhaps I shall never marry. The title could then pass to my younger brother, who has done just what I cannot."

Leonard's mouth curled at the corner. "You mean, he is wise and has married and produced a son," he said as Lord Repington sighed heavily. "Or is it now two?"

"It is two!" came the exclaimed reply. "My mother insists that I wed, but I do not think it necessary as yet." He sighed and picked up his brandy glass again. "Mayhap, when I am a little older, I shall feel the urge, but, as yet, I confess, I have no desire to do so." Setting down his now empty glass with a clink on the table beside him, he looked expectantly at Leonard. "Now, are you to accompany me to Lord Mowbray's? He has an evening assembly, which, I am sure, will still have many hours of entertainment ahead of it."

Leonard shifted a little uneasily in his chair. "I have no invitation."

"Nor I," Lord Repington grinned. "But Lord Mowbray is known for his lack of consideration for such things. No doubt, he will be glad to welcome us!"

This did not seem quite true to Leonard but, reminding himself that he was not to simply sit at Whites or sit at home but was doing what he could to find some enjoyment, he pushed himself out of his seat with an effort.

"Very well," he said as Lord Repington slapped him on the back in evident delight. "But I shall not stay too long. My first meeting with Miss Brooks—Lord Coulbourne's daughter—is tomorrow, and I should like to be at my best."

Lord Repington nodded in understanding. "Of course, old boy," he said. "Now, did you bring your carriage? No?" He chuckled. "Neither did I. A hackney it is to be, then! Come, Stafford. This evening shall be most excellent, I am quite certain of it!"

Unfortunately for Leonard, the evening was *not* as Lord Repington had hoped. Whilst his friend had been correct in stating that they would have no difficulty in joining the evening assembly, Leonard had soon found himself standing with a group of gentlemen who, like himself, seemed to have very little success in their attempts to dance with any of the young ladies present.

He sighed to himself as one of the other gentlemen in the group remarked upon one particular lady that was dancing. Leonard did not even look in the direction pointed out, for his interest in discovering the source of the gentleman's consideration was quite absent.

Turning away from the group, Leonard pushed aside any feelings of shame and embarrassment and kept his head high as he made his way towards a footman, who was holding a tray of drinks. He had assured himself that he would behave sensibly this evening, but now that he had seen the familiar looks of disgust etched on some ladies' faces, now that he had heard their polite refusal, Leonard felt nothing but embarrassment. Taking a glass, he brought it to his lips only to twist his face in disgust. Ratafia. It was not to his particular taste but, he considered, forcing himself to take another sip, it would certainly have the desired effect.

"Oh, excuse me!"

He turned at once, having been pushed forward by someone who had stumbled directly into him. Ratafia had splashed out a little from the glass, but it had not gone directly onto his jacket, for which Leonard was very grateful.

"Do excuse me."

A young lady and a slightly older lady, whom Leonard took to be her companion, stood in front of him. Her eyes were wide, and she was staring up at him, her face paling as she did so.

"There is nothing to be forgiven," he stated as the companion began to murmur something under her breath and pull her charge away slowly. "An accident, I am sure."

The young lady closed her eyes as though she could not bear the sight of him. "Indeed," she said, her voice wobbling. "You are very gracious, sir. Do excuse me." Her eyes flickered open, and she looked at him again, only to turn away swiftly, being hurried away by her companion who had clearly decided that Leonard was not suitable company for her charge.

Leonard dropped his head, aware of the all-too-familiar heat that climbed into his face. There always came that sense of shame, that sense of humiliation and indignity that swamped him every time someone looked at him that way.

"You are not leaving already?"

Lord Repington stumbled towards Leonard, clearly already in his cups.

"Yes," Leonard grated, his pain and upset hitting forcefully against the delight that was written into every line on Lord Repington's face. "I think I shall leave. There is nothing here for me."

Lord Repington put one hand on Leonard's arm. "My friend," he said, the smile fading quickly, his eyes focusing—with some difficulty—on Leonard's face. "Has something happened?"

Lifting his head, Leonard looked at Lord Repington and felt anger climb into his heart. Lord Repington could never truly understand. What he had at present, the freedom to do as he pleased and to go where he wished without judgment, without mockery, without shock or displeasure, was something that Leonard could never have.

"It is just as I should have expected," he spat, his words holding more ire than he had intended. "A lady looks at me and sees nothing but *this.*" His hand flew forcefully to his face as he gestured to the long, jagged scar that ran from just above his eye and down over his cheek, stopping just before his top lip. "They look at me and see the imperfection. Nothing more. I am either an object to be pitied or a picture of horror. I am nothing in between."

Lord Repington dropped his hand, his shoulders slumping as he tried to say something, but Leonard shook him off. He did not want to stay. Why had he ever agreed to come here? It was always going to be the same, always going to be just as he had come to expect.

"You see now why I must find a wife by arrangement rather than by choice," he said bitterly, turning away from Lord Repington. "A lady who will have no choice but to do as her father states—that is all I shall be able to achieve."

"Then I wish you success as you meet her tomorrow," Lord Repington said, his voice calm despite the fury that was busy eating away inside Leonard, the fury that must be very evident in both his words and his demeanor. "I am sorry, Stafford. I would not have asked you to come if I had ever thought."

"It matters not," Leonard stated, already beginning to walk away. "Goodnight, Repington."

He did not wait nor hear if his friend replied, concentrating only on making his way across the room and towards the door that would lead him to the outside and to freedom. His stomach twisted with mortification, his steps heavy with grief. This had all been a dreadful mistake and with it had come a deep, twisting fear that when he met Miss Brooks for the very first time tomorrow, she would look at him in the same way as the young lady had this evening—and as almost every other young lady had done in the past.

"Foolishness," he muttered to himself, jamming his hat firmly on his head and striding outside without even taking a moment to tighten his coat about him. Grateful that there was a hackney already waiting, Leonard climbed in at once and gave swift directions as to where he was to go. It was only when it began to pull away that he allowed himself to sit back, to feel a sense of relief beginning to swamp him. Finally, he was able to hide in the shadows, able to remove himself from all who would look at him with such dark fascination.

He should never have agreed to attend the evening assembly. It had brought only pain with it, a pain that Leonard had never once become used to no matter how often it bit at him. Sighing heavily, he closed his eyes. He had to remove this melancholy from himself as soon as he could, for tomorrow, no matter what it brought with it, was steadily approaching, and he could not appear as he was at present. Not if he wanted to make the very best impression he could on Miss Brooks.

"Let us hope she is not a harridan," he muttered to himself. "For I do not think I shall be given such an opportunity again."

CHAPTER TWO

"Ellen."

Ellen lifted her head and looked at her father as he walked into the room, setting her needlework down as a sense of dread began to creep into her heart. She had barely been able to have a moment's peace from her anxious thoughts as she struggled against the fear and worry about what her father would have to tell her. As yet, there had been nothing. Her father had breakfasted with both her and her mother but had remained fairly tight-lipped about what he had been doing, and Ellen herself did not even know whether or not he had been successful in his endeavors.

"Yes, Father?" she asked, placing her hands in her lap and lacing her fingers together. "Is there something the matter?"

He grinned at her and, instantly, Ellen's heart sank. There was no doubt in her mind now. Apparently, her marriage was to take place to a gentleman she had not yet even been introduced to.

"I was absent from the soiree last evening, Ellen, because I had important business to take care of," he told her, coming to stand closer to her and placing one hand on the back of a chair. "Your mother informed me that you probed a little more into where I was—although she did mention you were difficult about it..." For a moment, his smile faded and a slight frown flickered across his brow, but Ellen said nothing in return, forcing herself to remain silent to allow him to tell her everything at once.

"That shall be something you remove from your character," he continued with a firm nod. "However, as I was saying, you are aware as to where I went. I was speaking with a gentleman as to whether or not he would be willing to take you as a bride."

"And you were successful?" Ellen asked, resisting the urge to toss her head in frustration. "You have made the arrangement?"

"It is almost entirely settled," Lord Coulbourne replied with a chuckle. "He is coming here within the hour to meet you."

In an instant, it felt as though all of Ellen's insides had turned to liquid, and she had to press her fingers tight together to force herself to remain sitting upright.

"You are to greet him and converse with him with the greatest of politeness," Lord Coulbourne continued, although Ellen noticed that his voice had become a little more grave. "He desires very much to meet you before he will agree."

Ellen closed her eyes. "You mean to say that he wants to make certain I am not *very* plain," she said tersely, a sudden pain lancing her heart. "Is that not so?" Opening her eyes, she lifted her chin and looked defiantly at her father, who had begun to go a shade of red that warned Ellen she was pushing him a little too hard in her question.

It did nothing to prevent her from speaking so. Her father had to know how she felt, and there was nothing in her holding her back.

"That is *not* so, no," Lord Coulbourne stated angrily. "You are much too free with that tongue of yours, Ellen. *That* is what shall turn Lord Stafford away from you, not the fact that you are not particularly beautiful!"

The words stung, even though Ellen knew her father had not meant them to do so. She turned her head away and blinked back tears, feeling a hint of shame creep up within her heart.

"Lord Stafford is an excellent gentleman, Ellen," Lord Coulbourne said, his voice now gentle rather than angry. "I can assure you that I have spoken to him at length and he has every quality that I would expect. He will treat you well, Ellen. There will be nothing but a contented life as his wife."

Ellen took in a long breath but did not reply. Opening her eyes carefully, she turned her head to look back at her father, who was now gazing at her with an earnest expression, as though he wanted her desperately to believe him.

"Now, do you think you could be persuaded to return to your room and have that new maid of yours make certain that you are quite prepared for his arrival?" Lord Coulbourne asked, cajoling her along. "I know that this must have come as something of a surprise to you, but I give you my word that I am doing for you what I think is best."

Ellen swallowed hard and nodded, rising to her feet and making her way towards the door, safe in the knowledge that nothing she did or said would be of any particular use. If her father had decided this, then she could do nothing but obey. For a moment, she considered refusing to do as he asked, to behave terribly and without any sort of elegance during Lord Stafford's visit—but one glance up into her father's hopeful face and she knew she could not.

"This is for your good, my dear," Lord Coulbourne murmured, settling one hand on her shoulder as she passed. "Trust me, will you not?"

Forcing a smile, Ellen had to admit that what her father asked of her was not a particularly great trial. He had always been considerate of her and what she might need, and perhaps now, she had to have a little more faith in him.

"Yes, Father," she said softly. "Yes, I can do as you ask."

"Good." The relief in his face was obvious. "Now, do not be too long. I should like you to be waiting in the drawing-room when he arrives."

"You look a little upset, my lady."

Ellen glanced at her reflection in the mirror, taking in the dull eyes and the sadness that played about her mouth.

"I am," she admitted to her new lady's maid, Betty. "I am to meet my betrothed this afternoon."

Betty's eyes widened. "That is unexpected, then?"

Ellen let out a sad laugh. "Indeed, very unexpected," she said, looking at the maid in the mirror. Betty was there only for the Season, for Ellen had been in need of one and a friend had offered her the use of Betty for the few months she would be in London. Lady Coventry loved coming to London but was very soon to go into her confinement. Thus, Ellen had been given the wonderful resource that was Betty, and she was becoming all the more grateful for her with every day that passed.

"That is why we are to make you so presentable, then," Betty smiled, adjusting one of Ellen's curls. In the sunlight, her hair looked almost golden, Ellen considered, although the thought brought her no joy whatsoever. "I am sure that he will be very kind, Miss."

Ellen shook her head, making Betty frown almost instantly as she reached again to continue sorting Ellen's curls. "I do not think it will be as satisfactory as you anticipate," she answered heavily. "My father made it quite clear that he considers me plain and that, I am sure, will be one of the reasons I am to find myself wed to an older, uncaring gentleman."

Spearing Ellen's hair deftly with a pin, Betty placed one hand on Ellen's shoulder and smiled warmly at her. "It may not be as you fear," she said gently. "There now, you look quite lovely." Her smile lifted Ellen's spirits just a little, but still, the dullness in her eyes remained. "All you need do now is pinch your cheeks and you shall look quite lovely."

It was a balm to Ellen's heart to hear her maid say such a kind thing, even if Ellen herself did not quite believe it. Reaching up, she patted the maid's hand. "Thank you, Betty," she said, a trifle hoarsely given the sheer weight of emotion that rested on her soul. "Let us hope that it is as you say."

~

WAITING for Lord Stafford was an ordeal in itself. Ellen could not sit at peace, bringing both the ire of her mother *and* her father as she shifted her feet, picked up and then set down her needlework, rose to linger by the window and then, finally, to pace slowly around the room.

"Do sit quietly!" Lady Coulbourne chided, looking at Ellen with evident frustration. "You shall wrinkle your skirts."

"They will not wrinkle if I am standing, Mama," Ellen reminded her with a shake of her head. "I am not able to sit still at present. I must move about."

Her father opened his mouth—no doubt to reprimand her also—but at that very moment, a scratch came at the door, and in an instant, everyone froze in place.

The scratch came a second time, and Ellen found herself struggling for breath, such were her nerves. As though she were in a dream, she made herself walk back to her chair, hearing her mother's urgent whisper to do so, and sat down carefully, smoothing her skirts with shaking fingers.

Lord Coulbourne smiled broadly, giving no hint of anxiety, and rose to his feet.

"Come!"

Ellen's hands were shaking furiously by now, and she held them together tightly in her lap as the door opened.

"Lord Stafford, my lord," she heard the butler say, standing to one side as a gentleman walked through it and came towards them all.

"Lord Stafford!" Lord Coulbourne boomed, his voice filling the room. "Capital! Capital!" He turned and gestured to Ellen, who, realizing that she had not yet risen to her feet in order to greet Lord Stafford, hurriedly did so at once. She kept her eyes low, looking at the gentleman's chest rather than up into his face, fearful of what she might see. Would he be as old as she feared?

"Lord Stafford, might I present my wife, Lady Coulbourne—"

"Very glad to meet you," came the hasty reply as Lady Coulbourne curtsied.

"And," Lord Coulbourne continued, "my daughter, Miss Ellen Brooks."

Ellen sank into a curtsy, her gaze now fixed to the floor as she rose, her throat constricting, her stomach tight and all manner of fears assailing her.

You are being quite foolish, she told herself as her mother made to ring the bell for the maid and her father instructed them all to sit down again. *You must simply lift your eyes to his and take the gentleman in. What else are you doing but prolonging your agony if you do not?*

Taking in a steadying breath and reminding herself that she had courage within her yet, Ellen lifted her eyes and looked directly at Lord Stafford. What she saw astounded her completely—and it was just as well that no one was speaking to her and waiting for her to answer a question, for she was quite certain that she could not form a single word.

Lord Stafford was not at all as she had thought him to be. Her father had spoken truthfully, it seemed. He *had* given consideration to what she required and had not sought out an older gentleman to marry her off to. Instead, Lord Stafford was a gentleman who appeared to be close in age to herself, with a shock of brown hair that fell untidily over his forehead. His eyes were a vivid green, his gaze clear as he looked back at her with a hint of curiosity in his expression. There was no smile on his lips, and Ellen had the impression, from the way that he suddenly dropped his gaze and shifted a little in his chair, that he was not as confident as he otherwise appeared.

Her eyes drifted to his cheek, noting the scar that ran down one side of his face. She thought very little of it, for whilst most gentlemen of her acquaintance were perfectly groomed with no marks to distinguish them from others, she did not think it made Lord Stafford any less of a gentleman to bear such a scar. Nor did she think that she had any right to criticize or demean his appearance in any way, given that she was not of particular beauty. Idly, she wondered how he had come by such a thing, only to see that his brow was now furrowed as she caught his gaze again.

Her father was still speaking loudly, not allowing them any conversation, and thus, Ellen was able to look back at Lord Stafford without hindrance. His brows sat low, but his eyes searched hers, looking for something that she had no knowledge of. Ellen was certain there was a worry there, looking back at him without allowing her own expression to change in any way. What was it he wanted from her? Feeling a little awkward at his searching gaze, she allowed herself a brief smile and then looked away, not willing to study him to see if he returned it.

"My dear, the maid is at the door."

Lord Coulbourne stopped his monologue to bark something towards the door, although Ellen had to wonder how her mother had heard the maid scratch at the door over the sound of Lord Coulbourne's voice. This brought a glimmer of a smile to her lips and, much to her surprise, when she looked back at Lord Stafford, he was smiling too. The expression seemed to light up his eyes, his face no longer holding the strange anxiety that she had seen only a few moments ago.

Lady Coulbourne cleared her throat and nodded quickly to Ellen, who realized at once that she was being tardy in her duties. The maid had already set the tray down and was backing out of the room, leaving Ellen to serve the tea.

"Should you like some tea, Lord Stafford?"

They were the first words she had ever spoken to him, and, when he accepted, she found herself being very careful indeed with the task at hand. It could not be because she was drawn to the gentleman, for there was no immediate flurry of interest in her heart, but rather because, she realized, there was now a great deal of relief. Relief that Lord Stafford was as he now appeared and not as she had allowed herself to fear.

Handing him the cup, she let out a long breath and

smiled, noting how his eyes flared with astonishment and how it took a moment or two for him to return the gesture. Her heart quickened with anxiety for a moment, suddenly afraid that there was something about her that Lord Stafford disliked. Would she fail in the responsibility her father had asked of her? Would Lord Stafford inform her father that there was not to be a match after all?

Sitting down, Ellen folded her hands neatly in her lap again and made sure she was smiling gently. Much to her own astonishment, she was now afraid that something would go wrong with this particular arrangement. If it did so, then Ellen found herself worried that the next candidate her father put to her would be so entirely unsuitable that she would find herself broken with regret.

"Are you to attend Lord and Lady Dowding's ball tomorrow evening, Miss Brooks?"

Ellen blinked and then glanced at her mother, who nodded furiously.

"It seems I am to do so, yes," she answered, allowing a hint of amusement into her voice. "I confess, Lord Stafford, that I am not always fully aware of what invitations have been secured and where I am to attend. However, my mother is always able to guide me in such things."

Lord Stafford chuckled, and Ellen felt her heart settle into a calmer rhythm. "As any mother would, I am sure," he said, addressing Lady Coulbourne, who then blushed a little with the compliment. "Then mayhap, Miss Brooks, you might permit me to request a dance or two. It would please me greatly to have the opportunity to do so."

There was not even a moment of hesitation within her. "But of course, Lord Stafford," she said, aware of the broad smile that now settled on her father's face. "I would be very glad to do so."

Lord Stafford himself seemed pleased by this, for he smiled broadly and then looked away. "Wonderful," he answered, picking up his teacup. "I look forward to greeting you tomorrow evening, Miss Brooks."

CHAPTER THREE

Leonard could not help but grin as Lord Repington approached him, a look of expectation on his face.

"Well?" he asked as the crowd of guests swirled about them both. "You met with Miss Brooks, I hope?"

"I did," Leonard told him. "And before you ask, it went very well indeed!"

Lord Repington's shoulders dropped with evident relief. "Then you are satisfied with her?"

"Very satisfied," Leonard replied, remembering how he had looked into Miss Brooks' eyes, expecting to see the same horror, the same disdain that he had seen in others. However, Miss Brooks, although she had looked at his scar and had clearly taken note of it, had not reacted at all. He had wondered if it had been a controlled reaction on her part, knowing what her father expected of her, but he had found himself beginning to hope that she was just as she appeared. Her conversation had been confident and interesting, and whilst they had not spoken for an overly long duration, Leonard found himself eager to speak to her again.

"Then I am very happy for you," Lord Repington said with a smile. "I do hope that I can meet the lady in question myself this evening?" He looked all about him for a moment, as though he expected Miss Brooks to be standing somewhere nearby.

"She is not here as yet," Leonard laughed, feeling a good deal better than he had in some weeks when standing in the middle of a large social function. "But I shall be very glad to do so when the time comes. Although," he warned mischievously, "you are not to find yourself *drawn* to her, as you are with so many others."

Lord Repington arched one eyebrow. "You say, then, that she is beautiful? I thought her father considered her quite plain."

Leonard thought for a moment, then spoke honestly. "She is not a diamond of the first water, but I would not consider her plain," he said truthfully. "I think her very suitable in that respect." He smiled to himself as he remembered how she had appeared last evening, with her fair curls catching the sunlight that filtered through the window and the gentle smile that had tugged at her lips so often. There was a loveliness about her that was more than skin deep: he was sure of it.

"Then I shall do my very best *not* to find myself desperately in love with her," Lord Repington replied with a chuckle. "So, all is settled then?"

"Not as yet," Leonard admitted. "I will speak to her father this evening and state that I am more than contented with the match." He grinned, feeling quite contented. "By the end of the evening, all of the *ton* shall know of it!"

"And you shall have everyone speaking of the match for a time," Lord Repington replied with a grin. "But I am, as I have said, very happy to hear of your news. I am sure you will find great happiness with her."

Leonard smiled, looking at his friend and feeling a sense of certainty filling him. "I think we shall be very contented indeed," he said firmly. "Thank you, Repington."

"Then all is settled!" Lord Coulbourne exclaimed, slapping Leonard's shoulder. "The betrothal is agreed."

Leonard dared a glance at Miss Brooks, suddenly afraid that she would be frowning, displeased and unsatisfied. However, she was standing by her mother's side, the corner of her mouth curling upwards. Relieved, Leonard let out a long sigh and shook Lord Coulbourne's hand. "It is," he said with satisfaction. "Miss Brooks, might I see your dance card?"

She gave it to him willingly, their fingers brushing gently, and Leonard was surprised at the start the brief contact gave him. Quickly perusing the dance card, he took first the quadrille and then, feeling bold, the waltz. It had been some time since he had danced the waltz, and he feared now that he would not be able to do so with any sort of ease, but the opportunity to dance with his betrothed was not something that he could allow to pass him by.

"The quadrille first, Miss Brooks," he said, handing it back to her. "And then the waltz?"

"Most satisfactory," Lord Coulbourne said as Miss Brooks took the card back from him and, after a momentary glance at it, nodded and smiled, her eyes warm.

"I look forward to it, Lord Stafford," she said quietly. "I thank you."

"Why do you not take a turn about the room together?" Lord Coulbourne asked as Miss Brooks' eyes suddenly shot to her father's, her smile gone in an instant. "Since you are now betrothed, there can be no harm in it."

Leonard nodded quickly, thinking that he would grasp eagerly at the opportunity to speak to Miss Brooks alone. "I will return your daughter to your side very soon, Lady Coulbourne," he said, addressing the lady who was now staring at her husband as though he had lost his senses. "Although, if you wish to join us, then I should be glad of your company also." This, however, was not the truth, but it was, Leonard knew, the correct thing to say.

Lord Coulbourne's expression darkened with a slight frown, and it came as no surprise to Leonard that Lady Coulbourne quickly refused his request.

"No, I shall be quite contented to remain here and wait for Ellen's return," she said, smiling at him, although there was a flicker of uncertainty in her eyes. "I appreciate your consideration, of course."

Leonard bowed. "Of course," he said, before directing his gaze towards Miss Brooks. How strange it was to consider her now his betrothed! It had happened in the mere blink of an eye, and now he found himself an engaged gentleman. "Should you like to take a turn about the room with me, Miss Brooks?"

She stepped towards him at once, no hesitation evident. "But of course," she said in a clear, calm voice. "I would be glad to, Lord Stafford." When he offered her his arm, she took it straightaway, and they began to make their way slowly around the ballroom, careful not to knock into any of the other guests.

There was silence between them for a few moments. A silence that, Leonard had to admit, was a little awkward. He was not certain what to say, did not know how to begin to breach the quiet that now was separating them, feeling himself grow embarrassed by his own sense of failure.

"You are quite satisfied with me, then."

Astonished, he turned to look at her and saw, much to his surprise, a glint of humor in her eyes and a coy smile. Nervous laughter bubbled up within him, and before he could prevent it, some escaped from his lips— although it sounded a little more like a choked cough than laughter.

"Forgive me for being so blunt, Lord Stafford, but my father made it quite clear as to the reason for our meeting yesterday afternoon," Miss Brooks continued, amicably. "I will be entirely honest with you and state that I am glad it has all gone so well."

"Indeed?" he murmured, trying desperately to get hold of himself. "I am happy to hear it, Miss Brooks." Clearing his throat, he looked down at her again, seeing her calm expression and small, gentle smile. She seemed to be so at ease, so perfectly at peace, whilst inside, he was like a raging torrent of confusion. Why could he not think of what to say?

"I will tell you, Lord Stafford, that I have my faults, however," Miss Brooks continued when he said nothing more. "I hope my father has not pretended that I am quite perfect in every which way!"

This made him smile. "No, he has not," he said quickly. "He has been very truthful with me, and I with him. I have told him of my occasional irritability and my lack of patience with certain matters that I am quite decided upon." He chuckled, feeling himself grow a little more at ease in her company. "But I am sure that, whatever faults either of us possesses, we shall find a way to rub along well together."

This did not seem to please Miss Brooks, for she looked at him with a sudden sadness in her eyes that brought Leonard's smile crashing to the ground.

"I suppose he told you that I am very plain," she said, in the very same practical tone of voice that she had used only moments before. "And that I am, of course, stubborn at times."

Leonard did not know what to say. He was not used to a lady speaking with such openness and yet found it refreshing. There was, however, a glimmer of something unspoken in her eyes, perhaps a sadness that told him she knew all too well what her father had said of her.

"Does it matter what your father stated?" he asked, trying to choose his words with care so that she would not feel as though he agreed with everything that had been told to him. "I should very much like to discover more about you myself rather than simply believing what has been told to me." Feeling an urge to tell her a little more, Leonard drew in a sharp breath. "For example, Miss Brooks, I do not think you are at all plain."

Miss Brooks did not immediately react to such a statement. Instead, she continued to walk alongside him slowly, her head now drooping just a little and her gaze seeming to fix itself to the floor or to the feet of the other guests. Leonard began to panic that he had spoken foolishly, that he had said something that had now only upset her in some way. Frantically, he tried to think of something else he might speak of, something that might bring about a change in their conversation, only for Miss Brooks to lift her head and turn to look at him, her steps coming to a complete stop.

"I think you are very kind, Lord Stafford," she said, looking at him steadily, although her lips did not lift into a smile. "You speak honestly and with great fervor, seeking to lift my spirits and to ensure that I feel no sorrow. For that, I am truly grateful."

"I do mean what I say," he said with such fervor that Miss Brooks broke into a wide smile. "I mean every word, Miss Brooks. I think you quite lovely, in all respects—whether you are stubborn or not."

Miss Brooks' smile grew wider, and Leonard had the sense that his heart was lifting in his chest, filling with a new contentment and expectation as he looked back at his betrothed. It felt as though, for the very first time in his life, he had a chance of finding true happiness.

"Goodness, Lord Stafford!"

That sense of relief and anticipation left him in a moment as the harsh voice of one of his acquaintances reached his ears. Turning, he looked directly into the face of Lady Cartwright, who was looking at him with something akin to disdain.

"Whatever are you doing walking with a lady such as this?" she demanded, gesturing to Miss Brooks in an almost feverish manner, her hand holding her closed fan. "You ought to return a lady to her companion or to her mother the instant the dance is at a close. To keep her in your company—especially in *your* company, Lord Stafford—is quite unfair."

Leonard opened his mouth to speak, to retort, but had no opportunity to do so, for Lady Cartwright was then quickly joined by another, her lately married daughter who had, it seemed, come to remove her mother from the conversation.

"Mama," the young lady said, taking her mother's arm. "There is something that requires your instant attention."

"*This* requires my attention!" Lady Cartwright insisted angrily. "Lord Stafford has taken this young lady and will not return her to her mother!" Clicking her tongue loudly, she shook her head and, much to Leonard's horror, he saw a small crowd beginning to form around Lady Cartwright.

"Miss Brooks," he murmured, leaning a little more closely to her and speaking out of the corner of his mouth. "I think, perhaps, that it is time I took you back to Lady Coulbourne."

Miss Brooks glanced at him and, to his astonishment, he saw that her eyes were blazing with an anger he did not understand. Why should she feel any ire in this?

Lady Cartwright was being rude, certainly, but she was not speaking to Miss Brooks in any way.

"Do you hear those whispers?" Miss Brooks asked him as Lady Cartwright began to speak again. Leonard ignored her with an effort. "They are all speaking of you, Lord Stafford."

He tried to shrug. "Of course they are," he said without his nonchalance sounding at all genuine. "It is something I am well used to, Miss Brooks. I am not as perfect as a gentleman ought to be."

Miss Brooks rounded on him, her eyes wide with anger and her cheeks beginning to heat. "Just because there is something of insignificance upon your features, they believe they have a right to speak of you in such terms, to look upon you with disdain?" As she stared back at him, something seemed to dawn on her, and her mouth dropped open for a moment. "That was what you were expecting to see in *my* face also," she said hoarsely. "You thought that I would—"

"That is why I think that you and I shall do very well together, Miss Brooks," he told her as Lady Cartwright's voice became louder, clearly growing irritated that he was not listening to her as she believed he ought. "You are not as any other lady of my acquaintance. There was nothing of derision or worry or even disgust in your eyes. You saw my scar, and you accepted it without question and without judgment." He smiled at her, despite the worry that was rising within him about the unfolding scene that now surrounded them. "Shall I take you back to your mother now, Miss Brooks? I should hate to bring down their judgment upon me already."

Miss Brooks opened her mouth to acquiesce, then closed it again. Her brows lowered, and she shook her head, turning, instead, to Lady Cartwright. Much to Leonard's astonishment, she took a step closer to the lady and, in what was a strong stance, placed her hands on her hips and lifted her head.

"Is there a particular reason, Lady Cartwright, why you have come to speak to Lord Stafford so?" she asked, her voice seeming now to flood through the room, going over the tops of everyone's heads and drowning out the music that was playing. "He and I are simply taking a short turn together about the room, and there is no need for you to interrupt us in this manner."

A rumble of astonishment flooded the group around them, and Leonard wanted to step forward and pull Miss Brooks back, wondering if she had any understanding of what would be said of them both by the time this evening had come to an end.

"My dear young lady, I am only doing what is required," Lady Cartwright said in a pitying tone as though Miss Brooks did not understand what her actions meant. "You should be returned to your mother at once rather than being forced to spend more time in this gentleman's company."

The burst of shame that filled Leonard's heart was almost enough to make him drop his head again, but before he could do so, Miss Brooks turned back to face him, her eyes searching for his until she found them. A small smile lifted her mouth, and Leonard let out a breath he had not known he was holding.

"Perhaps it may surprise you, Lady Cartwright, but I

am quite contented in Lord Stafford's company," Miss Brooks said, in a slightly louder voice. "In fact, my mother *and* my father—Lord and Lady Coulbourne—are not only aware of my accompanying Lord Stafford, but they have actively encouraged it."

This brought yet another murmur of astonishment to the assembled group, but Miss Brooks was not finished yet.

"There is no need for you to step forward in this manner, Lady Cartwright," she said firmly. "Lord Stafford and I are quite contented in our conversation together, and he is, very soon, to take me back to my mother, who is waiting."

She turned and came to stand beside him again, leaving Lady Cartwright standing in a state of fury. Her cheeks had spots of color burning within them, her eyes were narrowed, and her hands were curled tight.

"Insolent creature!" Lady Cartwright exclaimed, throwing up her hands. "There is never any good reason for a young lady to continue in the company of a gentleman in the manner you are doing now! It is quite ridiculous."

"If my father has no objection, Lady Cartwright, then I cannot see why you should," Miss Brooks replied as one or two onlookers gasped at her audacity. "Now if you will excuse us, we have the rest of the room to walk through."

Lady Cartwright brandished her fan at Miss Brooks, and Leonard made to step forward, worried that the lady would hit his betrothed, but Miss Brooks remained steadfast, her hand tight on his arm.

"You are only going to spread rumors about your

conduct!" Lady Cartwright exclaimed. "Whispers will spread! Words will be spoken about you and the company you keep! Is that what you want, young lady? Is that what you desire?"

Miss Brooks laughed, and the sound shattered the dark clouds that surrounded them all.

"Lady Cartwright, I give no consideration to any rumors," she said brightly. "For they mean nothing."

"They will ruin your reputation!" Lady Cartwright threatened although Leonard knew full well that she spoke dire warnings that could not be true. "You will never find a suitable match should you continue to behave this way."

Again, there came that bright, tinkling laugh from Miss Brooks, and Leonard found his heart beginning to hammer furiously in his chest. There was an opportunity now for Miss Brooks to speak the truth, but he would not blame her if she did not, for their betrothal was of such a short duration that perhaps, even for Miss Brooks herself, it had not quite settled in her mind.

"I think you shall find, Lady Cartwright, that I have already made the most excellent match," Miss Brooks told her, her voice bright and clear as Leonard's heart continued to beat frantically. "In fact, your concern for my wellbeing and my reputation has come to naught, for there is nothing wrong in any way with a young lady walking with her betrothed." She lifted one eyebrow and glanced back at him, leaving Leonard struggling to smile as those who were watching not only gasped with aston-ishment, but immediately began to whisper to each other in a loud fashion.

"If you will permit us to continue," Miss Brooks finished, taking a step forward as Leonard forced himself to move, finding that his mouth was now curving into a smile, his heart thumping furiously with delight. "We should like to continue our short time together without further interruption. After all, it is important for a young lady to get to know her future husband as best she can before the wedding day. Do you not think so, Lady Cartwright?"

And with that final question, with that light, sweet smile on her face, Miss Brooks made her way past Lady Cartwright with Leonard by her side. He could not quite believe what had just occurred, what Lady Cartwright had said, and what Miss Brooks had done. It was quite astonishing, and yet, at the same time, utterly wonderful.

"I do hope you are not angry with my behavior, Lord Stafford."

Miss Brooks' smile had faded to nothing, her eyes now filled with worry as she looked up at him.

"I could not bear to have them all look at you in such a fashion, nor could I allow Lady Cartwright to speak in such an odious manner!" she exclaimed, shaking her head. "I am sure that I have only added to the many rumors and whispers that will now fly all around us, but I could not stand silently when such disparaging words were being pushed towards you."

Leonard shook his head, finding himself caught up with awe at how Miss Brooks had spoken.

"I find you quite marvelous, Miss Brooks," he told her, without hesitation. "I am not in the least concerned nor upset." Seeing the relief in her expression, he reached across and patted her hand. "In fact, I should like to thank you for your determination to combat such rude callousness. I have never had anyone do so before, and for that, I am truly grateful."

Miss Brooks looked back into his face, her expression serious. "You have had a little too much of such treatment, I think."

He shrugged, trying to pretend that it was not as serious nor as bothersome as it truly was. "It is something I have come to expect."

"Then I am sorry for it," Miss Brooks replied firmly. "And I can assure you that you shall never have such treatment from me. I shall not even ask you about it, Lord Stafford, for it is of little importance to me."

"Then I am all the more grateful for you, Miss Brooks," he answered as her face broke into a smile. "And I am quite certain that this match will suit us both marvelously."

"As am I, Lord Stafford," came the warm reply. "As am I."

CHAPTER FOUR

"I think that it all went very well indeed," Lady Coulbourne said, picking up her teacup and taking a small sip. Sighing happily, she set the cup back down and looked at her daughter. "Although I did hear that there was some sort of commotion with Lady Cartwright?"

Ellen had the decency to blush and hurriedly reached for her own teacup so that she would not have to answer her mother.

"Your father will want to know what happened," Lady Coulbourne said with a small shake of her head. "After all, Lady Cartwright is a highly respected—"

"She insulted Lord Stafford," Ellen interrupted, not allowing her flushed face to prevent her from speaking openly. "I could not simply stand there and allow her to do so!"

Lady Coulbourne's expression became one of surprise. "You mean to say that you felt the need to defend him?" She let out what was now a very heavy sigh, evidently a little frustrated that Ellen had felt the need to do such a thing. "I am certain there was no requirement for you to do so."

"I am certain that there was," Ellen replied stoutly. "How is Lord Stafford to know that I am willing to be both loyal and supportive of him as his wife if I do not speak out?" She felt the very same anger that had captured her last evening begin to do so again. "You do not know what was said, Mama. It was very cruel, and I did not like hearing it. I could not allow her to speak so, not when it was said in front of so many others."

Lady Coulbourne said nothing for a moment, watching Ellen speculatively, only to give her the tiniest of smiles, her eyes flickering with sudden mischief. "I presume, then, that Lady Cartwright was surprised to hear of your engagement?"

Hearing the mirth in her mother's voice, Ellen looked at her in surprise, only to smile herself. "I do not mind telling you, Mama, that I very much enjoyed seeing the look of astonishment on her face," she said, a sense of pride filling her. "There was something pleasant in being able to do so."

Lady Coulbourne chuckled, then seemed to stop herself with an effort. "I should be chiding you, should I not? And yet, I confess a little satisfaction of my own in hearing of Lady Cartwright's shock. She should not speak to you in such a manner, Ellen!"

"I am certain she will not do so again," Ellen replied with a smile. "There is nothing you need fear, Mama. The *ton* will, no doubt, be speaking of my engagement for a few days, given just how spectacularly it was announced, but Lord Stafford and I are quite prepared for such a thing."

"Then, you are pleased with your father's choice?" Lady Coulbourne asked gently, only to be interrupted by a scratch at the door. She glanced towards it but did not call out, returning her gaze to Ellen and waiting in evident expectation of an answer.

"I am contented, Mama, certainly," Ellen admitted, quietly. "And also greatly relieved."

"I am glad," Lady Coulbourne replied, settling back into her chair with a look of quiet contentment. "And I must say that I am proud of your willingness to defend your betrothed in such a way, Ellen. I have always thought you to be a little outspoken, but in this case, I think you have done well."

This, Ellen considered, was something of a compliment, and she accepted it as such, smiling to herself as her mother called for the butler to enter.

"My lady," the butler murmured, stepping inside and bowing. "You have a visitor who would like to spend a few minutes with you if it is permissible."

It was not quite time for afternoon calls, and Lady Coulbourne glanced at Ellen in surprise, who merely shrugged and picked up her needlework.

"Might I see the card?" Lady Coulbourne asked as the butler came towards her. She picked it up, perused it, and then let out a gasp of delight.

"Oh, indeed!" she cried as Ellen looked up from her sewing. "Send Lady Newfield in at once! I would be very glad indeed to see her."

"Lady Newfield, Mama?" Ellen asked, setting her

needlework down and then rising to her feet. "I do not think that I—"

"A very old and very dear friend," Lady Coulbourne exclaimed, rising to her feet and brushing down her skirts. "Come, Ellen, stand up at once!"

There was no time to protest, no time to ask any further questions. Instead, Ellen had only a second or two to set down her needlework and then get to her feet, looking expectantly towards the door. An older lady came in, her eyes finding Lady Coulbourne's face in a moment.

"Lady Newfield!" Lady Coulbourne exclaimed, holding her hands out as she hurried forward. "You are in London at last!"

Lady Newfield laughed, her blue eyes twinkling, her gray hair neat and elegant, giving her a somewhat refined appearance.

"I have been in London these last few Seasons but have found myself quite caught up with a few matters," she answered, turning to look towards Ellen. "Else I would have come to you much sooner."

Introductions were made, and Ellen curtsied quickly before being instructed by her mother to ring the bell for tea and refreshments. Thereafter, she sat back down again, turning her attention to her needlework and allowing her mother and Lady Newfield to speak at length. From what her mother had said, Lady Newfield was a dear friend of her mother's, even though Ellen had never once met her.

"I believe the last time we met was when you were in London with your son," Lady Newfield remarked, reminding Ellen that she had not always been by her mother's side. In fact, when her parents had been fixed upon the idea of making certain their son was happily married, she had been left at the estate in the care of an older aunt whilst her mother, father, and brother had all gone to London without her. That must have been when Lady Coulbourne and Lady Newfield had last met.

"I am here again for my daughter's sake," Lady Coulbourne said, spreading out one hand towards Ellen. "Although, much to my relief and my contentment, she is already betrothed and, within a few short weeks, shall find herself the wife of one Lord Stafford."

This did not appear to either please nor surprise Lady Newfield in any way, for she only nodded and smiled rather than make any remark.

"The betrothal was only announced yesterday," Ellen added, a little irritated by Lady Newfield's manner. She was unable to say anything further, however, for the door was scratched, and in came the maid with the trays for them all. Lady Newfield laughed, smiled, and conversed with the two of them, although mostly Lady Coulbourne, before, finally, she decided to take her leave.

"You must come to dinner with us this evening," Lady Coulbourne said firmly. I know that it is very late to ask you such a thing, but if you have no prior engagements, then I must insist."

Lady Newfield laughed and nodded. "I would be glad to join you," she said as Ellen rose to her feet to bid the lady farewell. "And now, I *must* take my leave, for I am certain you will have a good many callers, and I shall not like to hold you back from them."

"It has been very good to see you," Lady Coulbourne answered with such a bright smile that Ellen could not help but feel warmth towards Lady Newfield for bringing her mother such joy. "And I look forward to this evening. Good afternoon to you both."

"AND YOU SAY that she is a friend of your mother's?"

Ellen nodded, speaking to Lord Stafford quietly as they sat at the table with the other guests. "Mama spoke about her at great length once she had departed," she said, glancing at Lady Newfield, who was now speaking to another of their guests. "They have been writing to each other for years, it seems, although they have not been in each other's company regularly." She smiled. "I am very glad to see my mother so contented. She has always had something to worry about, something to concern herself with, but now, finally, there is nothing at all for her to become anxious about."

Lord Stafford chuckled. "You mean to say, it is because you are now betrothed, your brother is settled, and all is just as she has hoped it to be?"

"That is it precisely," Ellen answered with a smile. "I think, also, that she is pleased that I am so contented." There came with those words a swell of heat the lifted from her chest and rose to cover her face. "I feared, Lord Stafford, that you would be a much older gentleman who would have very little regard for me other than seeing me as a means to continue the family line."

She thought for a moment that he might laugh aloud

but, instead, his eyes shuttered for a moment, and his mouth pulled firm.

"I have seen that happen before," he told her, a frown suddenly darkening his brow. "It does not please me."

This gratified Ellen in a way she could not explain. It was, perhaps, a realization that Lord Stafford was a man who was very upright in his thinking, who would not abide certain things and certainly would never press such situations on either herself or upon any future children they might come to have. It was a strange thought, but one that made her relieved. She would never have to worry that her children would not be well taken care of by their father. He would have their best interest at heart.

"But I am glad that I was not as you feared," he continued, his smile returning and lighting up his features. "And we shall have to discuss when the wedding shall take place. I will, of course, take care of the arrangements and have the banns called as is expected."

A blush warmed her cheeks again, but she held his gaze, finding her heart quickening just a little at the thought of being his bride. There was no time to discuss anything at present, however, for Lord Coulbourne quickly announced that the port would be served—and Ellen had no other choice but to rise to her feet with the other ladies and make her way from the room.

"I think you have made an excellent match, Miss Brooks," said one of the other ladies present, as they walked towards the drawing-room. "Lord Stafford appears to be an excellent gentleman, although I confess I am not particularly well acquainted with him."

"Nor I, as yet," Ellen replied with a smile, her eyes

twinkling. "But like you, I have considered that he is a very amiable gentleman indeed. I am certain I shall be very happy. I—"

"Miss Brooks!"

A sudden exclamation came from behind her, and Ellen turned at once. To her astonishment, Lady Newfield, who had been the very last to leave the dining room, hurried towards her whilst the rest of the ladies continued on their way.

"Yes, Lady Newfield?" Ellen asked, a little alarmed to see the way Lady Newfield's eyes had widened, a touch of paleness about her cheeks.

Lady Newfield captured Ellen's arm. "You must come with me at once, Miss Brooks," she said urgently. "Your father has taken ill."

Ellen did not move forward but rather found herself stumbling as Lady Newfield tugged at her arm. "What do you mean?" she asked, wondering if this was some sort of ruse. "I have only just left the dining room. I—"

"As I made to leave the room, I turned to see your father slumped in his chair with one or two gentlemen leaping out of their chairs to go to him," Lady Newfield exclaimed, her words urgent and her eyes wide. "We must not trouble your mother yet, of course, for it may be nothing more than a little too much liquor, but I feel that someone ought to be with him."

Ellen caught her breath, hearing the anxiety in Lady Newfield's voice and realizing at once that she was speaking the truth.

"Where did they take him?" she asked as Lady

Newfield led her back towards the dining room. "The parlor? It has an adjoining door to the dining room."

"I believe so," Lady Newfield said, allowing Ellen to lead the way. "I do hope that it is nothing serious, Miss Brooks."

Finding herself unable to answer given the anxiety settling deep within her, Ellen pushed her way into the room to find Lord Stafford, Lord Armstrong, and another gentleman she could not quite recall the name of standing around a chaise.

"Miss Brooks."

Lord Stafford was beside her in a moment, his hand gentle on her arm.

"What happened?" Ellen whispered, seeing her father lying on the chaise, unmoving and with his eyes closed. "He was doing very well only a few minutes ago."

"I cannot say," Lord Stafford answered, keeping his voice low as though Lord Coulbourne would be able to hear him. "One moment, he appeared quite all right. And then, his mouth seemed to twist to one side, his eyes became fixed, and the next moment, he had collapsed in his seat."

Ellen closed her eyes against the rush of tears that threatened to overwhelm her. "We must send for a doctor."

"I have instructed the butler to do so already," Lord Stafford said as Lady Newfield nodded in agreement. "I hope that was not inappropriate."

Shaking her head, Ellen found herself grasping Lord Stafford's hand, feeling herself grow suddenly weak as a coldness washed over her, her skin gooseflesh.

"I should inform your mother," Lady Newfield murmured, but Ellen shook her head.

"No, allow the evening to continue at present," she said, hoping that Lady Newfield would understand. "If we alert everyone to what has occurred, then there will be such a furor that the *ton* will be whispering about it for many, many days, and I cannot allow such a thing to happen." Taking in a deep breath, she tried to gain hold of herself, knowing that she had to be completely in control despite the circumstances. "Lord Armstrong," she continued, her voice a little stronger now. "Might you inform the other gentlemen that my father is quite all right and that he has simply drank a little too much whisky?" She knew that such a thing was nothing more than an outright lie, but she was doing so in order to protect her father. "I will not have gossip being spread about him, and I must hope that you will all understand my reasons for doing so."

The gentlemen all nodded their agreement, with murmurs of understanding coming from their lips.

"Indeed, you may inform them that Lord Coulbourne will be taking to his bed in order to recover, but that the evening will continue as planned," she stated firmly. "Lady Newfield, might you go and inform my mother of what I have said? I should not like her to be overwhelmed with fear as yet. The doctor may say that it is nothing more than a sudden faint that he will soon recover from."

Lady Newfield nodded, her hand pressing gently to Ellen's arm for a moment. "But of course."

Ellen took in a shaking breath, making her way closer

to her father. He appeared so different from what she knew of him. Normally he was full of life, his eyes bright and his voice booming out towards her. Now, he was pale, his skin appearing a little waxen, and his eyes tightly closed. Were she not able to see the rise and fall of his chest, Ellen was sure that she would not have believed him to still live.

"I will stay with you, if you wish," Lord Stafford murmured as Ellen found herself leaning into him, wanting to find some sort of comfort and going towards him without even thinking. "Whatever you require, Miss Brooks, I will do what I can to provide it for you."

Ellen nodded, swallowing hard as she turned towards him. She went into his arms without hesitation, her head resting on his shoulder as sobs began to shake her form. It took a moment, but Lord Stafford soon had his arms around her, holding her close as she began to cry. The shock had been great, and she needed to allow herself to express the swell of emotion that was steadily growing within her.

"It will be quite all right, Ellen," Lord Stafford said softly, no eagerness to do anything other than hold her for as long as she required it. "You will not be alone, and I am quite sure that your father will recover in time."

Ellen closed her eyes tightly and sniffed, aware of the dampness on her cheeks. "Thank you, Lord Stafford," she whispered as fresh tears began to well in her eyes, her pain growing steadily as she dared another glance at her father. "I must hope that it will be as you say."

CHAPTER FIVE

I t had been three days since Lord Coulbourne had taken ill. Lady Newfield, he knew, had taken up residence in the Coulbourne house, mostly so that she might be a support to Lady Coulbourne. For himself, he had gone to see Miss Brooks every day, but she had appeared sad and wan each time he had called. The worry on her face over the illness of her father had been more than evident, and Leonard felt entirely unable to help her. There was nothing he could do or say that would aid her through this difficult circumstance other than to be present with her and try his best to inject a little encouragement into her life.

"Take this letter to Miss Brooks," he said as the servant came into his study. "There is no need to wait for a reply."

The servant, Briggs, nodded and took the letter at once, leaving quickly without a word. Leonard always used the same servant to deliver his letters and knew that

Miss Brooks would be fully aware that it was he who had written to her should she catch sight of the man from a window. He hoped that what he had written would bring her even a little relief, feeling a trifle guilty that he was to go out into London society this evening when she, no doubt, would be resting at home with her mother, father and Lady Newfield, in the hope that there would be some sort of recovery.

There came a scratch at the door.

"My lord," the butler murmured after Leonard had called for him to enter. "Lord Repington is present, and his carriage is waiting."

Leonard nodded, feeling not even the slightest eagerness to make his way out of his townhouse, but, with a heavy sigh, he made his way to the door and left the room.

"HE IS NOT RECOVERED, THEN?"

Leonard shook his head as the carriage trundled towards the evening soiree that they were to attend. "I remained with Miss Brooks and Lord Coulbourne until the doctor arrived," he told his friend. "The doctor stated that there was an apoplexy of sorts, which is why Lord Coulbourne's mouth appeared at such a strange angle before he collapsed." He lifted one shoulder in a half-shrug. "I believe he has regained consciousness but finds one side of his body very weak indeed. He is, however, eating a little and is having the very best of care." A frown marred his brow as he recalled what Miss Brooks had told him of her father's condition. "The doctor wished very much to bleed Lord Coulbourne, but Miss Brooks herself would not hear of it and, to my very great surprise, Lady Newfield agreed with her."

Lord Repington looked at him askance. "But surely Lady Coulbourne would—"

"Lady Coulbourne is very anxious indeed and has given all decisions on her husband's care to Miss Brooks and to Lady Newfield," Leonard answered with a shake of his head. "The poor lady is very distressed."

"Then you think Miss Brooks correct in her decision?"

Thinking for a moment, Leonard shook his head. "I cannot say, for I have not seen Lord Coulbourne myself as yet. But if Miss Brooks and Lady Newfield believe that he is too weak to have such a thing done, then I shall respect their opinion on the matter."

Lord Repington made a non-distinct sound in the back of his throat but said nothing to either agree or disagree with what Leonard had said.

"I do hope that he will recover fully, however," Leonard finished, a little uncertain as to what he should say next. "It is a terrible ordeal for them all."

"Of course," Lord Repington said hastily, as though he feared Leonard believed him to be quite unconcerned. "It does sound most dreadful." He tipped his head. "Does this mean that the plans for your wedding must wait?"

Leonard nodded, aware of the wretchedness that filled him at such a thought. "They must, yes," he answered softly. "I do not much like the idea, for it means that I shall have to wait longer to wed Miss Brooks, but I understand entirely the reasons for doing so." The carriage came to a stop and both he and Lord Repington prepared to climb out. "I will wait for as long as is necessary, but I will not change my mind."

Lord Repington chuckled as the carriage door was held open for them. "I should think not, given just how very lovely your Miss Brooks is," he said before stepping outside. "I heard about what she said to Lady Cartwright." Again, another chuckle came as Leonard came to stand beside him. "You will not find another lady like Miss Brooks, not if you looked through all of London!"

"I am glad you approve," Leonard replied with a grin. "But yes, you are quite correct. Thus, I shall wait for her for as long as I must, knowing just how blessed I am to have found such an excellent match."

THE EVENING SOIREE was not as quiet as Leonard had expected. He had thought there would be a decent number of guests but nothing particularly overwhelming. However, he was utterly astonished to discover that the room was practically filled with ladies and gentlemen, who stood together in tightly packed groups as yet more came to join them.

"Good gracious," he murmured, having greeted their host for the evening. "Does Lord Dunstable realize just how many people are within?"

Lord Repington grinned and gestured to a door that Leonard had not yet seen. "Lord and Lady Dunstable pride themselves on having such a great number of guests that it is very hard indeed to move about their rooms," he told Leonard, who had been entirely unaware of such a thing. "Lord Dunstable has already opened the adjoining music room and, in time, will have the library available for anyone wishing to play cards or the like." Laughing at the expression on Leonard's face, he picked up a glass of brandy and handed it to him. "It will not be as bad as it appears, Stafford. Once the library is opened, it usually becomes a very pleasant evening."

Leonard shook his head in disbelief. "I presume, then, that you have been at this particular event before?"

"Twice," Lord Repington replied with such a sense of pride that he had both attended and survived the occasion that Leonard could not help but laugh. "Go on, now, enjoy the evening."

"If I can," Leonard muttered, his mood suddenly darkening. He made certain to attend such occasions, for he would not allow society's unfair judgment of him to push him aside. Instead, he came out just as was expected, knowing full well what he would face but finding the strength within himself to ignore the looks and the whispered remarks.

"Ah, but I am certain things will have changed for you now," Lord Repington replied with a gleam in his eye. "I should not be very surprised indeed if those here this evening wish to speak only of your betrothal to Miss Brooks." He nodded sagely as Leonard threw him a doubtful look. "Mark my words, things will be very changed indeed."

"I must hope so," Leonard remarked, disbelief filling him as Lord Repington saluted him with his glass of brandy and then made his way towards a group of ladies, which, Leonard was sure, would contain whatever particular young lady had captured his attention of late.

Sighing to himself, he turned around and made his way slowly through the guests, finding no one of particular interest to speak to. Not that he found such a thing worrisome, for he did not mind waiting to find someone of importance rather than drowning in idle chatter that meant nothing at all.

"Lord Stafford, I had been hoping very much that I might see you here."

Something jolted hard within him. That voice. He knew that voice very well, indeed. It was a voice he had never wished to hear again, a voice that had thrown his life into complete disarray. Everything within him screamed to keep walking, to ignore it entirely so he would not have to pay it any attention, but he knew he could not do such a thing.

"You will not speak to me?"

He turned, looking the speaker directly in the eye. "I have no wish to do so, as you well know." His voice was hard, his whole body burning with a searing fire. "I am surprised that you should be so eager also."

There came no immediate response. "I have come to lay claim to you."

Scoffing, Leonard shook his head, praying that no one

around them would hear the conversation, praying that their own chatter would make them deaf.

"You have no claim upon me," he stated with as much firmness as he could. "There is nothing that you need to say to me. There is no reason for us even to be meeting in this fashion."

"You mean to say that I cannot come to London, simply because you are present also?"

Anger poured into his heart, but Leonard controlled himself with every bit of strength he possessed. "You are welcome in London, but you need not come to seek me out," he stated forcefully. "You know all too well that our acquaintance is at an end. That was your choice, and one that I have paid for dearly." His brows knitted and his hands curled into fists. "Good evening."

"I do not think our conversation is finished."

He threw a disparaging look over his shoulder. "It is."

"But what of your scar?"

Leonard froze. There were only two people in all the world who knew the reasons for his scar: his shameful, hateful reasons why he now bore the mark of it on his face. And one of those two was now standing near to him. What was it she was threatening to do? To reveal all to the rest of society?

The voice came closer. His eyes closed tightly, and he fought to keep his anger, his shame, and his fear pressed down, worried that should he speak with anything other than calmness, he would reveal himself to everyone within the room.

"I have already told you, Stafford, that I have come to lay claim to you." The voice was gentle, but Leonard hated every word that was said. "You owe me that, do you not?"

"I owe you nothing." He rounded on the lady, looking down into her green eyes and seeing the cunning smile on her face. "You have already deceived me once. I shall not allow you to do so again."

The lady shrugged one shoulder, turning her face away from his. "I had you desperately in love with me, did I not?" she asked softly. "I believe you swore me fealty."

"I swore loyalty to someone I did not know," Leonard answered harshly, no longer concerned as to whether or not anyone could hear him. "You have no right to demand anything from me."

She tipped her head, her beautiful face expressionless and cold. "But I have your word and the promise given to me," she said, reminding him of what he had done. "You have the scar from your determination to prove your love for me."

Fear tightened his heart, but he ignored it completely. "And then you threw such loyalty in my face. You told me nothing but mistruths, deceiving me at every turn. You never once cared for me. You used me as a plaything that you could discard."

She sighed heavily as though he were deliberately obtuse. "I will not turn away from this," she told him, taking a small step closer to him and speaking with such infinite gentleness, such evident care, that Leonard could barely breathe. It was all so familiar and yet so disturbing to his heart. He wanted to move back from her but could not do so, such was the crowd of guests. Instead, he turned his head away, refusing to look at her any longer, showing her that he had no interest in conversing with her.

"There are things that you can and shall do for me if you do not wish to hold to the promise you once made," she said quietly. "I shall not allow you free of that vow, Stafford. Requests I make shall be granted without hesitation."

"You are foolish in your demands," he hissed, turning his eyes towards her despite his intention not to do so. "Do you think that I shall so easily bend?"

Her smile was bright, her eyes sparkling, but there was a cold hand that reached in and grasped his heart. Shuddering visibly, Leonard turned his head away again, making to move past her, only for her hand to capture his. Shaking it off, he glared at her again, knowing that if he did not leave her side instantly, then he would say something or perhaps do something that would bring him so much shame and regret that it would not be worth his staying in London.

"If you do not, then there shall be consequences, Stafford," he heard her say. "I have your letters. I have your gifts. I have your word, given to me with tears. I know of what you did. I know everything. And should you refuse, then all of society shall know of it too."

The words clung to him like dirt and, try as he might, Leonard could not brush them off. Making his way through the crowd, he forced himself to swallow in great gulps of air in an attempt to calm his thundering heart. Just when had she come to London and how, in heaven's name, had she managed to make herself known to Lord Dunstable?

"I see you were speaking to Lady Moore, Lord Stafford!"

The voice of Lady Dunstable reached Leonard's ears, and he was forced to stop, even though his head was buzzing with thoughts, sweat breaking out on his brow. The lady smiled at him, her eyes searching his face as a little uncertainty began to make its way into her expression.

"Y—yes, yes," Leonard managed to say, doing all he could to behave as normally as possible, even though he was drowning in both fury and fear. "Lady Moore is someone I have known for a long time, Lady Dunstable, although I have not spoken to her nor even seen her for some years." *And for very good reason,* he thought to himself grimly as Lady Dunstable's smile grew. "You are acquainted with her?"

Lady Dunstable waved a hand. "I have only been introduced to her recently, Lord Stafford," she said by way of explanation. "I have heard her sad tale of her late husband's demise and am very sorry for it." Sighing, she shook her head. "It is always very difficult when a lady is left to fend for herself."

"Indeed," Leonard muttered, knowing all too well the gentleman that Lady Dunstable spoke of but not wanting to give any indication that he did. "And she is returned to London to seek a new husband, then?"

A slight flush of color rose in Lady Dunstable's cheeks. "I could not say, Lord Stafford!" she exclaimed, clearly thinking him a little rude for asking such a blunt question. "She has never spoken to me explicitly about such a thing, although..." Seeming to consider for a moment, she moved a little closer and dropped her voice low. "Although she has confided in me that Lord Moore has left her with very little, and that the new Lord Moore has been very ungenerous towards her." Shaking her head in obvious disapproval, she sighed and patted Leonard's arm. "But I should not like you to tell anyone else of such a thing, of course. I speak of it only because I know that you are long acquainted with her and must be, of course, concerned for her."

It was an effort not to contradict the lady. "Indeed," he muttered, wishing desperately that he could find a simple way to end this particular conversation. "I am sure she is very grateful that you were good enough to include her in this evening's occasion, Lady Dunstable."

"Oh, but it was nothing at all," Lady Dunstable replied with a small smile. "But I must hope that, from this one evening, she will make many new acquaintances and find herself further involved in society. That would be very satisfactory indeed."

"Yes, very satisfactory," Leonard echoed, a sense of dread flooding over his heart.

"But I must go," Lady Dunstable finished, finally freeing him from their conversation. "There are one or two guests that I have not yet said more than a few words to, and I should not like to fail in my duties." With a warm smile, she excused herself and allowed Leonard to go.

Closing his eyes for a moment, Leonard dragged in air and then forced himself forward, making his way to the door. He had no desire to be there any longer, not when *she* was present.

"Stafford!"

Leonard did not turn his head, did not even acknowledge Lord Repington's call. Instead, he continued making his way through the guests, elbowing one or two out of the way and ignoring the exclamations of shock or pain that came from them. He cared nothing for them, cared nothing for Repington or for Lord Dunstable's soiree. All he wanted was to return to his own townhouse where he might find enough brandy to ensure he did not remember this night until, at least, the following morning.

"Where are you going, Stafford?"

A hand touched his elbow, but Leonard shook it off. "I must go, Repington," he growled, not looking back at his friend. "I am sorry, but—"

"What has been said to you this time?" Lord Repington sighed, sounding almost irritated that Leonard was finding this evening to be difficult also. "Has it been another look of disdain? Another exclamation of horror?"

Leonard stopped dead, angry beyond measure. Turning slowly, he jabbed one finger into Lord Repington's chest. "I am sorry if you find my presence a burden, *friend*," he said, gritting his teeth in an attempt to control his fury. "I must apologize if you find my struggles and my pain to be a heavy weight upon your soul. Perhaps, therefore, it *is* best if I remove myself so that you can enjoy the evening without worrying as to how I fare."

Lord Repington's eyes went wide. He looked down at where Leonard's finger had pressed into his chest before frowning hard.

"Whatever is the matter, Stafford?" he said, his voice now holding concern rather than a tired irritation. "I did not mean to suggest that your company is any sort of burden." He spread his hands. "Perhaps, like you, I find the remarks, the comments, and the harshness of society to be a little wearying, that is all."

"It is not directed at you!" Leonard exclaimed, fully aware that everyone around them could hear him speak so but finding himself entirely unable to control his voice. "You are able to go through society without hesitation, without *provocation*, whereas I must endure and endure and endure without ceasing! There is nothing more I can do but listen and accept what is said to me, the looks that are thrown at me. How can you possibly even *begin* to understand what it is like? You enjoy society to its fullest. I am pushed towards the edges."

This was not, of course, the true reason for his anger, for his upset and his frustration, but Leonard was not about to tell Lord Repington the truth. He had kept that part of his life, that part of his past, entirely to himself for a long time, and he certainly was not about to start sharing it now. The threat that she held over him was real, and Leonard could feel the strength of it tugging at him, pressing at him until he feared he might buckle under it.

"I—I am sorry," Lord Repington said slowly, looking at Leonard as though he had lost his senses. "I have never meant to come across as uncaring or inconsiderate, although I presume now, from your reaction, that I must have done so." A flash of anger appeared in Lord Repington's eyes, and he drew himself up to his full height, his chin lifting and his brow furrowed. "Do excuse me. I must return to the society that I evidently love so ardently, instead of standing here conversing with you about what has troubled you so greatly that you are determined, yet again, to return home." Swallowing once, Lord Repington shrugged. "I hope you have an enjoyable evening at home, Stafford. Do excuse me."

Leonard felt his shoulders sink as he watched Lord Repington depart, suddenly very aware that he was now standing alone. He had not meant to speak cruelly to his friend but had, he saw, done precisely that. Lord Repington had come to ensure that he was not deeply upset, was not discouraged or the like, and instead of being grateful for his friendship and consideration—which had long been a part of Leonard's life—he had allowed his anger to burn through him and pour out of him in harsh words. The urge to go after his friend and to apologize for what he had said began to tug at him—but then, much to his horror, he saw Lady Moore making her way towards him. Her eyes glittered as they fixed themselves to him, and Leonard turned on his heel, desperate not to be in her company. The door was a welcome escape for him, seeming to pull him towards it, and Leonard stepped through it eagerly. He did not stop walking until he had reached the main door, hurrying out into the night and the cool air. He allowed himself three long breaths before he set off down the street.

Whatever was he to do? He was entirely alone in this, unable to speak to anyone about Lady Moore and her hold over him. Had she truly the intention to ruin him in so complete a fashion if he did not do as she demanded?

Miss Brooks.

Leonard stopped walking, his heart hammering furiously as he considered his betrothed. If she should ever hear of Lady Moore, should she know of what he had done, then she would be injured more than anyone. Society would whisper of her as well as of him. They would state that surely, she had known of it and would mark her foolish for being willing to accept him regardless. The way they would look at her, the way they would speak of her...it was something that he could barely allow himself to think of. He had endured a good deal of shame himself, knew very well what such a circumstance felt like, and the thought of it being placed on Miss Brooks' shoulders as well was something he could not allow himself to consider.

Closing his eyes, Leonard let out a loud groan as he dropped his head into his hands, the sound echoing down the street. Everything had disappeared from him in an instant. He had been so happy with Miss Brooks, had been eagerly looking forward to planning their wedding, his mind filled with thoughts about his future with her by his side. And now, it had been shattered by the presence of Lady Moore.

Dropping his hands to his sides, Leonard lifted his head and stared out into the dark street. There was nothing but shadow and gloom, and, as he began to walk again, he felt the darkness reaching out to him, pulling him in against his own will. The past had come back to him, taunting him, ridiculing him, and making him feel useless, powerless, and weak.

There was nothing he could do to fight it. Lady

Moore, the lady he had once thought to be kind, so generous of heart, and upright in her thinking, was nothing more than a dark spirit whose cloak of deception was once more wrapped around him—and there was no easy way of escape.

CHAPTER SIX

Ellen smiled at her father as he looked back at her from his comfortable bed. There was no return smile on his face, although she was certain that his mouth appeared a little less slack than before.

She *knew* she had been correct in demanding that there was no bloodletting. Whilst she knew all too well that it was what was expected, there had been something in her father's eyes when the doctor had suggested it that had made her refuse. Her mother was quite happy to leave the decisions to Ellen, being so distraught with the illness of her husband that she felt unable to make wise decisions.

"Good afternoon, Father," Ellen murmured, sinking into a chair placed beside her father. "You look a little recovered today."

That was true, at least. There was not as much paleness to her father's cheeks, although there was a weariness in his features that Ellen thought would take a long time to leave. "You have been eating, I hear?"

Her father closed his eyes and, with an effort, nodded. "Soup," he slurred, the words coming out of the side of his mouth. "Bread." He did not seem to be contented with how he had pronounced the second word and tried to do so again and again until Ellen reached out and touched his hand.

"I am glad you have eaten," she said softly, realizing that she was holding her father's limp hand rather than the one he was able to use without difficulty. "And you are resting, just as you should." Smiling at him, she reached for the book she had been reading aloud to her father every afternoon. "Shall we continue?"

Her father's lips curved up on one side, his eyes closing quickly, and Ellen felt her heart lift with hope. There were small but significant improvements with her father. When his fingers pressed the back of her hand as she held it—a light finger touch, barely perceptible— Ellen felt tears burn in her eyes. Her father was doing all he could to get better, to recover from this apoplexy, and she was so very proud of his strength.

"Let me read, Father," she whispered, not trusting her voice as she opened the book with one hand as it rested on her lap, trying to find the correct place. Taking a moment, her vision blurred as she looked down at the page, she finally cleared her vision and then began to read.

～

"How does he fare?"

Ellen let out a long breath and smiled at Lady

Newfield. She knew that her eyes were a little red-rimmed and that she must look upset, but it was from relief rather than sorrow.

"I think he is improving, albeit very slowly," she told Lady Newfield, who pressed both her hands to her heart in evident gladness. "His hand—the one that has no strength, pressed mine for the briefest of moments. His speech was clearer, although he said only a few words." She smiled and sat down in a chair. "He is sleeping now."

"I am sure he was glad to have you read to him, to have your company," Lady Newfield said softly. "Your mother will sit with him once he has woken, as she always does."

Ellen, who had seen very little of her mother, looked at Lady Newfield. "How does she do?"

Lady Newfield smiled sadly and sat down. "This must be very strange for you, Miss Brooks. To have a veritable stranger come into your home and not only reside with you but converse, eat, and sit with you." She sighed. "I did not expect to be needed so, but I am glad to be here. I do hope that you do not feel any upset over my presence."

"No," Ellen answered honestly. "I do not feel any such emotion, Lady Newfield. To be truthful, I am very glad that you are with us at present. My mother would not have managed without you, I think." Lady Newfield, she considered, seemed to exude a calmness that went through the house in its entirety. Ellen's mother had gone to Lady Newfield with her sorrow and distress, and Lady Newfield had been able to comfort her in a way that Ellen knew she never would have been able to do. She felt no frustration or irritation at this, however, but a true sense of gladness and relief that Lady Newfield was as willing and as capable as she had been thus far.

"That is good, for I should not like to cause you any further difficulties than what you face at present," Lady Newfield said with a smile. "You are doing very well, Miss Brooks, under the circumstances. There is a courage and a strength within you that is more than a little evident and will do you good in the coming days."

Ellen smiled back at the lady, thinking that she could now understand what had made her mother so delighted to see Lady Newfield again. The lady had a kindness of spirit and a goodness of heart that was evident in almost everything she said or did—and such characteristics were not found in a good many people.

A scratch came at the door.

"My lady," the butler murmured, looking directly at Ellen. "Lord Stafford calls upon you."

Ellen's heart lifted in a moment, her eyes brightening and her heart quickening. "Thank you," she said, making to get up—but Lady Newfield was already on her feet.

"You remain. I shall depart," she said with a quick smile. "Although I will send in your lady's maid."

Nodding, Ellen rose and brushed down her skirts, just as Lord Stafford was shown into the room. Lady Newfield greeted him quickly and then left the room, the door remaining ajar.

"Good afternoon, Miss Brooks."

"Good afternoon, Lord Stafford." She stepped forward and reached to take his hands—something she had been doing since the day her father had taken ill—but much to her surprise, Lord Stafford took a step back. His brow furrowed, his eyes dropping to the floor, and he placed his hands behind his back, shuffling his feet a little as he did so.

Ellen's heart dropped.

"Miss Brooks, I have come with only one intention," he said, his voice low and grating. She did not recognize his voice, nor his dark expression. Lightly, she pressed one hand to her stomach, a deep, unrelenting fear taking hold of her, making her tremble visibly.

"It is my sorrowful intention to bring our engagement to an end," Lord Stafford continued after a few moments of silence. "There is nothing to be done, Miss Brooks. I am sorry."

Her mouth refused to move as she stared at Lord Stafford, trying to find something to say, some question to ask of him—but her mouth would not move, and she simply could not form the words to ask him what he meant. Their betrothal had only just taken place, and, since then, they had spent many hours talking, laughing, and seemingly enjoying each other's company. Had they not both expressed gladness for their match, for their betrothal? Why then had he now come to her with this?

"I am sorry, Miss Brooks...Ellen, I do not mean to..." He trailed off, closing his eyes tightly and then dropping his head. She heard him groan but still could not respond to him, feeling tears burning in her eyes as she stared blankly ahead, seeing the torment in his expression and feeling nothing but pain.

"I have to do this," he ended up saying, lifting his eyes to hers, coming closer to her and standing helplessly before her. "It is for the best, Ellen. Truly. You will find happiness with another."

She closed her eyes, and a tear slipped onto her cheek.

"I must appear to be the most awful of men; mayhap I am," Lord Stafford muttered, pushing one hand through his hair. "I cannot continue in good conscience with our betrothal, Miss Brooks, no matter how much I—" He stopped himself with an effort, his eyes closed again as a heavy breath issued from his lips.

"I do not want to find happiness with another."

Ellen's first words to him were nothing more than a broken whisper, tears beginning to flow steadily down her cheeks now.

"We were contented, were we not?" she asked, finding herself filled with desperation instead of anger. "There was gladness on both our parts. We found a joy with the match that I am certain I shall never find with anyone else." Her hand reached out and rested lightly on his shoulder, her whole body shaking with the shock of what he had said to her. "I do not understand why you would want to break apart something that we had both deemed to be so...wonderful."

Lord Stafford began to reach up to her hand, only to pull himself back. "It is for the best," he said brokenly. "I cannot explain more. I—I am sorry, Miss Brooks."

Ellen was filled with fright, with a desperate urge to keep him with her. If he left now, then she was sure he would leave her side for good. Before he could react, before he could turn away, she had put her arms about his neck, pulled herself close, and kissed him.

For a long moment, he did not react. Ellen kept her eyes closed, kept herself precisely where she was—and then she felt him soften. His arms went about her waist, his head tilted just a little, and he kissed her tenderly.

"No."

Lord Stafford wrenched himself from her, his face hot and his eyes darting from place to place, seemingly unable to fix upon her.

"Please, Stafford," Ellen whispered, her hands falling helplessly to her sides. "I have already begun to care for you. You have been a tower of strength to me these last few days. We have begun to form a bond, have we not?"

She looked at him desperately, wanting to reach out to him but worrying that he would not accept her should she do so. That kiss had been one of the most astonishing and yet beautiful moments of her life, confirming to her that she had, indeed, begun to feel a closeness towards Lord Stafford that she worried would now be pulled away from her without her consent. Society would know that he had cried off. They would look at her and wonder what she had done. Rumor would be rife. But worst of all, she would lose the happiness that had only just come to her, the hopes for her future that had begun to build within her, the joy that had started to fill her heart. Lord Stafford was going to take it all away and she still did not understand why.

"We have formed a bond," he admitted, hanging his head. "Which is why it brings me all the more pain to have to remove myself from you, to sever the bond that is between us."

Ellen closed her eyes and knew she had lost him. He

was going to do this regardless of what she had said, regardless of what had just happened between them.

"Please know that I have found myself feeling the way you have just described, Miss Brooks," he said, his tone becoming a little more severe, no longer as broken with emotion. "Do not ever think that I have found myself wishing to bring this to a close while thinking that I have made some sort of mistake. I have never once had a momentary regret. It brings me great pain to do what I must."

"Will you not tell me of it, Lord Stafford?" she asked, holding out one hand to him, a thin flare of hope still burning in her heart. "Will you not speak to me of whatever it is you are enduring at present?"

Lord Stafford looked back at her steadily, his green eyes flickering with uncertainty—and for a moment, Ellen believed that he might do as she had asked. She began to hope that the truth would be spoken and that she would understand—only for him to shake his head and turn away.

"Farewell, Miss Brooks," he said, his voice heavy with grief. "I—I am sorry."

The door was pulled closed behind him, leaving Ellen standing alone in the room, staring at the door with mounting horror. At any moment, she expected him to return, to suddenly pull the door open again and to rush towards her, to pull her into his arms and to tell her that he was sorry, that he had been mistaken, that he had been foolish.

Nothing happened. Instead, Ellen found herself shaking furiously, her limbs suddenly weak as she fought to remain standing. She could not understand what had happened, nor why Lord Stafford had done such a thing.

"Miss Brooks?"

The door opened, and Ellen lifted her head, her eyes dulled as she saw Betty standing in the doorway.

"You needed me?" Betty asked, frowning as she came closer to her mistress. "Is—is something the matter, Miss Brooks?"

Closing her eyes, Ellen felt tears run down her cheeks again, heard Betty's exclamation, and felt her arm about her waist as Betty led her slowly towards a chair. She sat down heavily, her eyes flooded with tears still as the maid went quickly to fetch her mistress a brandy.

"Take a sip, Miss Brooks," Betty murmured, bending down low and pressing a glass into her hands. "Please. It will do you good." She watched Ellen anxiously, waiting until Ellen obediently lifted the glass to her lips, taking the smallest sip of the brandy.

She closed her eyes. The brandy was restorative, yes, but it did not take away her pain. In fact, it seemed only to make her more aware of it, more settled upon it.

"I should fetch your mother," Betty said worriedly, looking into Ellen's pale face. "You need someone with you at present."

"Not my mother."

The maid, who had started towards the door, turned around and looked at Ellen in confusion.

"Not my mother," Ellen whispered, before lifting her glass and taking another sip. Closing her eyes, she waited until the warmth from the brandy swept through her. "If you must fetch someone, then seek out Lady Newfield."

The last thing Ellen wanted was for her mother to be disturbed, not when she was already busy and upset over Lord Coulbourne's illness. And yet, there was a desire not to be alone, to speak of what had happened to someone—and thus, her thoughts immediately turned to Lady Newfield.

"At once, my lady." Her expression was a mixture of confusion and anxiety, looking back at Ellen again for a long moment before she pulled open the door. Ellen said nothing, staring blankly ahead and barely hearing the words that the maid spoke to the footman outside. And then, Betty was back in the room, coming to crouch beside Ellen as she encouraged her again to take a sip of the brandy.

"Is there anything I can do?" Betty asked, her concern for Ellen reaching out in comfort, but Ellen swiftly shook her head. There was nothing her maid could do. There was nothing anyone could do. Lord Stafford had made his decision, and there appeared to be nothing that Ellen could do to change it. Reaching out, Betty took one of Ellen's hands in her own and pressed tightly. No words were spoken, but there was still comfort there. Comfort that soothed Ellen's broken heart just a little.

"Ellen!"

Lady Newfield rushed into the room without hesitation, holding her hands out towards Ellen. Ellen did not move but looked up at the lady, her lips quivering with the effort of maintaining her composure.

"What has happened?" Lady Newfield cried, looking

announced, but Lord Stafford and I are quite prepared for such a thing."

"Then, you are pleased with your father's choice?" Lady Coulbourne asked gently, only to be interrupted by a scratch at the door. She glanced towards it but did not call out, returning her gaze to Ellen and waiting in evident expectation of an answer.

"I am contented, Mama, certainly," Ellen admitted, quietly. "And also greatly relieved."

"I am glad," Lady Coulbourne replied, settling back into her chair with a look of quiet contentment. "And I must say that I am proud of your willingness to defend your betrothed in such a way, Ellen. I have always thought you to be a little outspoken, but in this case, I think you have done well."

This, Ellen considered, was something of a compliment, and she accepted it as such, smiling to herself as her mother called for the butler to enter.

"My lady," the butler murmured, stepping inside and bowing. "You have a visitor who would like to spend a few minutes with you if it is permissible."

It was not quite time for afternoon calls, and Lady Coulbourne glanced at Ellen in surprise, who merely shrugged and picked up her needlework.

"Might I see the card?" Lady Coulbourne asked as the butler came towards her. She picked it up, perused it, and then let out a gasp of delight.

"Oh, indeed!" she cried as Ellen looked up from her sewing. "Send Lady Newfield in at once! I would be very glad indeed to see her."

"Lady Newfield, Mama?" Ellen asked, setting her

need to do such a thing. "I am certain there was no requirement for you to do so."

"I am certain that there was," Ellen replied stoutly. "How is Lord Stafford to know that I am willing to be both loyal and supportive of him as his wife if I do not speak out?" She felt the very same anger that had captured her last evening begin to do so again. "You do not know what was said, Mama. It was very cruel, and I did not like hearing it. I could not allow her to speak so, not when it was said in front of so many others."

Lady Coulbourne said nothing for a moment, watching Ellen speculatively, only to give her the tiniest of smiles, her eyes flickering with sudden mischief. "I presume, then, that Lady Cartwright was surprised to hear of your engagement?"

Hearing the mirth in her mother's voice, Ellen looked at her in surprise, only to smile herself. "I do not mind telling you, Mama, that I very much enjoyed seeing the look of astonishment on her face," she said, a sense of pride filling her. "There was something pleasant in being able to do so."

Lady Coulbourne chuckled, then seemed to stop herself with an effort. "I should be chiding you, should I not? And yet, I confess a little satisfaction of my own in hearing of Lady Cartwright's shock. She should not speak to you in such a manner, Ellen!"

"I am certain she will not do so again," Ellen replied with a smile. "There is nothing you need fear, Mama. The *ton* will, no doubt, be speaking of my engagement for a few days, given just how spectacularly it was

Ellen up and down as though she feared she was injured. "Where is Lord Stafford?"

"Gone," Ellen said flatly, her eyes drifting towards the door. "He does not mean to return."

Lady Newfield blinked in surprise, looking to Betty, who could only shake her head.

"Then the engagement?"

Closing her eyes, Ellen held back her sobs. "It is at an end," she said hoarsely. "It is all at an end. There is nothing more for me here." Opening her eyes, she looked back into the startled face of Lady Newfield. "Lord Stafford has brought our engagement to a swift and brutal end."

CHAPTER SEVEN

To walk away from Miss Brooks had been one of the most painful things Leonard had ever done. The words he had spoken had burned his heart, had seared his throat and caused him such pain that it had been too much to endure. He had been forced to stop, forced to close his eyes, and draw courage within himself to do what *had* to be done.

There had been no other choice. Lady Moore was much too dangerous a foe to be allowed close to Miss Brooks and, even though he had to admit that there was a warming affection for her within his heart, there was nothing he could do to continue on with their betrothal. In order to protect her, to keep her from any shame, sorrow, and overwhelming pain, he had to pull himself from her before it became all the worse.

Having spent the last three days in his townhouse, mulling over what he had done and allowing the very same pain and sorrow to overtake him over and over again, Leonard found his spirits becoming weak. He did nothing other than sit in a chair in either his study or drawing-room, his brandy close to him should he need it. And, every day without fail, he received two letters. One from Miss Brooks, brought by her lady's maid, whilst the other came from Lady Moore.

Today was no different.

The letters sat quietly in his lap but Leonard did not look at them. He had read each one every day since they had first begun to arrive, but today he did not have the energy to do so. He knew what would be said. Lady Moore would demand to know why he was not writing to her, reminding him of the power she had and the threats that now hung over his head. She told him expressly what she wanted and expected him to give her, but Leonard had done nothing in response. The letters from Miss Brooks tore at his heart and sank him all the lower into his melancholy. Her letters were long and feverishly written, begging him to explain to her what the trouble was and why she had been pulled away from him so. Her words of affection were clear, repeated with such a determination that it was as though she wanted to engrave those words upon his heart so that they might never be forgotten.

"I cannot forget you, Miss Brooks," he whispered, his throat burning with agony as he ran one finger over the yet unopened letter. "I do not think I ever shall."

His eyes closed, and he was swamped with the memory of her kiss. The way she had stepped forward and pressed herself into his arms had quite overwhelmed him. Recalling how he had been entirely unable to react at first, how he had stood, unmoving and astonished, a sad smile tugged at the corner of his mouth. The astonishment had given way to wonder, which in turn had been replaced with a tremendous sense of joy. His arms had wrapped around her waist, his head had tilted, and he had kissed her desperately, as though she were the only source of life and he a man close to death.

And then, he had forced himself to step back. He had seen the hope in her eyes and had known he would have to extinguish it again. Pain tore into his heart, and he closed his eyes, groaning aloud as he bent forward, his head in his hands and his elbows resting on his knees.

"My lord?"

Summoning every bit of strength he could, Leonard looked up to see the butler just at the door.

"You did not hear my knock," the man said apologetically. "But you have a visitor, my lord."

Leonard shook his head. "I am not inclined towards visitors today."

"But you shall see me regardless," came a familiar voice, just as Lord Repington strode through the door past the butler, who protested weakly but then, with a look of relief in his eyes, shut the door behind him.

"It seems my staff fear for my welfare," Leonard said bleakly as Lord Repington strode to the brandy and, instead of pouring a glass as Leonard had expected, picked up the decanter and took it to the other side of the room. "For heaven's sake, Repington, whatever is it you think you are doing?" Frowning in frustration, he picked up his brandy glass and quickly threw back the rest of it out of fear that Lord Repington would take it also before slamming it back down hard on the small table beside him.

"So, we are in a foul mood?" Lord Repington said, sitting down in a chair opposite Leonard and looking at him with a steady gaze. "Or is it that you are unwell?"

Leonard grimaced. "Neither."

"Then it is to do with Miss Brooks," Lord Repington said, his expression now darkening somewhat. "Pray, tell me that the rumors of your engagement coming to an end are nothing more than idle gossip!"

Lifting his eyes to Lord Repington's face, Leonard shook his head. "It is true," he said hoarsely. "I have cried off."

For a long moment, nothing was said. Lord Repington did not react but instead continued watching Leonard with a steady gaze, his eyes searching his face.

"You care for Miss Brooks, do you not?" Lord Repington asked. "I was certain that you—"

"Pray, do not torment with your questions!" Leonard exclaimed, cutting Lord Repington off as he swiped the air with his hand. "I cannot even begin to explain just how much pain this has caused me."

Lord Repington frowned, but there was no anger there. Instead, there came that familiar expression of concern that Leonard knew so well. Leonard looked away, fully aware that he had a great friend in Lord Repington but still having very little desire to explain all that had gone on.

"I shall not do as you ask."

Leonard's head shot up.

"Nor will I vacate your house until you tell me the truth of what has occurred," Lord Repington continued, his expression now grave and his voice low. "I was so very glad to see you contented with Miss Brooks. This last sennight, you have been happier than I have ever seen you!" He shook his head. "But now you have brought your happiness to a sharp end for seemingly no reason at all and have sunk into a very obvious and upsetting despondency."

Shaking his head, Leonard tried to find the words to say that he did not want to cry off, but instead found himself unable to speak. There was, he realized, a small part of him that *did* want to share all with someone, even though he knew very well that there would be a great deal of shame that came with it.

"Please, old friend," Lord Repington said, sitting forward in his chair. "I can see that you are quite broken by this. I swear to you that there shall be no judgment and no criticism on my part."

"I am—" Leonard stopped himself, closing his eyes for a moment. "You say that you shall not criticize, shall not judge, but I swear to you that when I tell you all, you shall see me in a very different light."

"That will not matter," Lord Repington said emphatically. "Do you think that there are not things I am ashamed of? Things that I have kept hidden and would prefer to remain so?" He shrugged and sat back in his chair. "I am all too aware that the gentleman I am is not the gentleman I ought to be. The way that I quicken from one young lady to the next, without having any intention of settling my heart upon any of them is, I know, both selfish and foolish."

"This is not a matter of mere foolishness," Leonard muttered darkly. "But if you insist—and I know you well enough to be aware that you shall sit there for the rest of the day and the night if you have to—then I shall speak to you the truth."

Lord Repington said nothing, remaining precisely where he was and looking at Leonard with a steady gaze. Fearing that his friend would turn his back on him the moment he learned the truth, Leonard took in a deep breath and forced himself to begin.

"You are quite right, Repington. I have been very contented of late. I have been very happy with the match and indeed, with Miss Brooks." His heart began to ache, but he did not stop. "In fact, I should admit that I have come to care for her. If things had continued as they were, then I am certain that I would have had a great deal of affection for her—and, if I were blessed, she with me." His eyes closed. "I was looking forward to our wedding day, making plans for our future together. And then, I saw Lady Moore."

Lord Repington said nothing but rose to his feet and fetched himself a glass of brandy as Leonard watched on. Lord Repington did not, however, give a glass to Leonard himself, which, Leonard considered sadly, was probably for the best.

"You may be surprised to learn that I have become acquainted with Lady Moore," Lord Repington said suddenly, astonishing Leonard. "When you left the evening assembly—an evening we need not discuss, so do not even think to begin to do so—I was introduced to her."

Leonard shook his head. "No doubt by design," he muttered heavily. "Lady Moore most likely saw you speaking with me at length and wanted to make certain that she was, thereafter, introduced to you." He shrugged, aware of the spark of anger in his chest. "It is just another way for her to exert her control."

Lord Repington let out a sigh, rubbing his forehead with one hand. "I thought her very charming," he said, speaking with great honesty. "In fact, I had thought to call upon her and—"

"You have not done so, I hope?" Leonard interrupted, a sense of panic catching his heart. "You have not yet visited her?"

It took a moment, but Lord Repington eventually shook his head. "I was to go this very afternoon," he said slowly. "But of course, as I have already said, I shall not do so now."

Leonard's smile was wan. "I am grateful," he said heavily. "And relieved that you would be so willing to remain." Shaking his head to himself, he sat forward in his chair, placing his elbows on his knees and joining his hands together, lowering his head so that he would not have to look at his friend. This next admission would be very painful.

"Lady Moore is someone from my past," he said, inwardly demanding that the words come forth. "She is a creature most terrible, but I have not always known her to be."

"You mean, you once thought her lovely, with a very fine character," Lord Repington suggested as Leonard nodded. "She certainly is beautiful, Stafford. You cannot be blamed for thinking that of her."

"But it is more than that," Leonard said before he

could hide behind Lord Repington's words. "When I knew the lady, she was Miss Henrietta Sinclair."

Taking a swig of his brandy, Lord Repington nodded but said nothing further.

"She was nothing more than the niece of Lord Russell and did not have any claim to importance other than that. She had no wealth, no dowry—nothing at all. And yet, during our first meeting, I believed myself to be completely in love with her. My heart was lost, I told myself. I could barely eat nor sleep due to the thought of her." He shrugged. "We met many times during that summer, and I believed myself to be quite attached to her, even though I knew I could do nothing about such a matter."

"I see," Lord Repington murmured, still looking a little confused. "And this was when you had taken the title?"

Leonard shook his head. "A little before then," he admitted. "I was a young man, and she a very young lady. I ought not to have thought any such thing of either her or myself at the time, but even then, even at that young age, she was already ensuring that her many wiles were being put to good use." His heart sank as he recalled his own foolishness, but he continued on regardless. "Of course, my father would never permit me to engage myself to a lady who had nothing, and thus, I did my level best to remove her from my mind."

"Which was wise indeed," Lord Repington said slowly. "I presume you achieved such a thing?"

Shaking his head, Leonard confessed a little more. "I struggled to do so, Repington. I could not seem to chase her away. My first thought in the morning was of her; my final thought before I slept was of her. And then, my father passed away, and I took the title, accompanied with the period of mourning that I then undertook."

A look of understanding came into Lord Repington's eyes.

"During my mourning, a letter came from Miss Sinclair," Leonard continued, fully aware that he was exposing his pain all over again but knowing that he had no other choice. "She expressed her sorrow at the loss of my father and wrote such pretty words in such a delicate hand that I felt myself begin to yearn for her company all over again." One hand lifted by way of explanation. "Given that I was caught up with all manner of considerations relating to my title, my new responsibilities, as well as my own grief, I had been able to, for the first time, lose all thought of her. But her letter, you understand, began to burn a renewed sense of affection for the lady deep within my heart."

"Understandably so," Lord Repington murmured, no judgment in his voice. "I know very well that the lady has a fair countenance and could easily use all that she has to encourage affections within a gentleman."

Leonard dropped his head, aware of the shame that was beginning to flood him. "I began to write to her," he said slowly. "In fact, we began to correspond a great deal. I learned that her own father was very near death and that she was very much afraid of what would become of her. It was, from what I understood, only she who remained in the family, for her mother had passed away many years ago, in giving birth to the second child, a son.

Her uncle had already married and, it seemed, cared very little for Miss Sinclair. I was certain that Lord Russell would come to her aid, but Miss Sinclair no longer felt sure of that connection nor the affection she believed Lord Russell once had for her."

"That seems strange," Lord Repington remarked quickly. "Were you not a little concerned by such a thing?"

Spreading his hands, Leonard looked directly at his friend. "I believed every word she said," he told him bitterly. "I had no reason to think that she did not speak the truth. Thus, I trusted that when she told me that Lord Russell was to take his own daughter to London for the Season and had said specifically that he could do nothing for Miss Sinclair at present, I believed her."

Waiting in silence for a few moments and fully expecting Lord Repington's judgment to be thrown down upon him, Leonard was all the more surprised when Lord Repington shrugged and rose to fetch more brandy.

"I can see why you would think such a thing," he said, adding another measure to his glass. "Such a statement would make sense, would it not? It is very reasonable indeed for a gentleman to think only of his daughter rather than his niece."

Rather glad that Lord Repington seemed to understand, Leonard let out a long breath and dropped his head. "This is where you will think very ill of me, however," he said hoarsely. "After the Season ended, and once my mourning period was over, I thought to go and visit Miss Sinclair. I did not know what would become of such a visit, but I could not very well leave her stranded in such difficulty alone. However, when I wrote to her of my plans, she sent back a short note stating that her father had died and that she did not know what would become of her. That was all it said."

Lord Repington sat back down heavily in his chair. "You were anxious, I should think."

"I was frantic!" Leonard admitted. "I thought myself in love with the lady! I wanted to ensure she was protected, that she was safe and secure. Now, I did not know where she was or what had become of her! I wrote to her many, many times over the next few months, but never once did she reply." Lifting his eyes to Lord Repington's, he saw the curiosity burning in his friend's eyes and knew that he was, by now, fully invested in the story. There was to be no escape for him now. "I was frantic with fear," Leonard admitted, dropping his hands and flinging himself back into his chair. "I could do nothing but think of her. My heart quailed, and I found myself regretting every moment when I could have spoken to her of how I felt, when I could have written to her of my emotions but chose not to do so."

A look of sudden understanding came into Lord Repington's expression. "And then she wrote to you?"

Leonard closed his eyes. "She did," he said hoarsely, recalling just how much his heart had cried out with relief and joy on that day. "I still remember reading every word furiously, believing myself to be blessed beyond measure to have heard from her."

Nodding slowly, Lord Repington tilted his head a fraction, his eyes curious. "What did such a note say?"

Leonard bit his lip, aware of the heat that now rose

into his face. "It stated that she was quite alone. Her father, it seemed, had many illegitimate children, and such a thing had only become known once he had passed away. Her uncle, Lord Russell, being quite horrified to discover such a thing, had turned his back on her completely and left her with nowhere to go. The house was no longer hers to live in. The possessions within were sold, giving her a little coin, but once such funds ran out, she did not know what she would do."

"And you, of course, made to help her," Lord Repington added slowly. "Did you seek to send her money?"

"I did more than that," Leonard whispered, his face hot. "I rode to where she was staying and paid for a carriage to take her back to my estate." Dropping his gaze so that he would not see his friend's astonishment and, perhaps, his immediate displeasure that Leonard would have done such a thing, Leonard shook his head furiously.

"Upon reflection, it was not the wisest of actions," he said hoarsely. "But my intentions were good. I thought to marry her, to make her my bride, so that she would not suffer any further pain."

A heavy breath came from Lord Repington, and Leonard lifted his head, daring a glance at his friend. Would there be scorn on Repington's features? Would he despise him for what he had done?

"You mean to say," Lord Repington murmured, his eyes open and no distaste pulling at his mouth. "You mean to say that you had Miss Sinclair *residing* in your house, without chaperone, without—"

"And now you know my shame," Leonard broke in as Lord Repington's brows flew upwards, his eyes rounding with astonishment. "My only defense is that I fully intended to marry the lady within a few short weeks, and she, when I put it to her, confessed that she had come to love me. Her heart, it seemed, was entirely my own. My happiness knew no bounds."

Lord Repington blew out a long, slow breath, shaking his head as though he could not quite believe it.

"I—I did not go to her," Leonard said hurriedly, for fear that Lord Repington would think the worst of him, even though what he had done was foolishness in itself. "I never once approached her. We—we may have shared kisses, but in every other respect, I was a gentleman to her."

"I quite understand, truly," Lord Repington said, surprising Leonard entirely. "You had the best of intentions, and where else was she to go?"

Closing his eyes with relief, Leonard nodded slowly. "You are very gracious in your judgments," he muttered, rubbing one hand over his eyes. "But even now, there is more to this sad tale that I must now express."

Lord Repington spread his hands. "I am ready to listen without judgment," he said, making Leonard smile ruefully. "In truth, this matter intrigues me, for I must understand what went so disastrously wrong between you both. It sounds as though you were to be quite the contented match."

Leonard ran one hand over his face, preparing himself to speak words he had never once told to another living soul. It was his shame, his heavy burden that he had thought he would always carry alone—except now, he was to share it with another.

"The marriage was set to take place," he said softly. "I gave Miss Sinclair my word that I should marry her. She begged for me to write such words down, to make her the promise again, so that she might always have it to hold." One shoulder lifted. "I thought it a very...tender request, and thus, I made the promise in writing. I believe," he continued, wincing as he spoke, "I told her that if I was unable to wed her, I should always stand by her side and give her whatever she required so she would never again have to be in such a state of loneliness and fear. I embellished my words and my promises a great deal, Repington. I thought that we would wed and all would be settled."

"I see," Lord Repington remarked, his brow furrowed and a darkness seeming to spread across his features. "No doubt you gave her gifts."

"I gave her many," Leonard admitted, closing his eyes as he recalled just what he had done. "Items of great value, items that meant a very great deal to me. One of them was, I am sorry to say, a gold locket. I had a miniature placed inside and had words of love engraved on the back."

"Goodness," Lord Repington muttered, shaking his head. "Then you made quite sure that she knew of your affection and your love for her."

"In all the ways I could," Leonard confessed. "The day of our wedding drew near and then, as I was walking out through the gardens, a gentleman suddenly approached on horseback."

Again, Lord Repington's expression filled with astonishment. "A gentleman?" he repeated, surprised. "Was it Lord Russell?"

Leonard shook his head. "It was a gentleman I had never met before in my life," he said, recalling the surprise that had filled him when the man had leaped from his horse and brandished a sword in his face. "I did not know his name, nor why he had come to my estate. I made to speak to him, but the man demanded to know where Miss Sinclair was and stated that I had no other choice but to give her to him at once."

"Good gracious!" Lord Repington exclaimed, his eyes all the wider. "What did you do?"

Again, embarrassment flooded Leonard. "I thought that he had come to steal Miss Sinclair away, to force her to marry someone that Lord Russell had chosen for her. After all, Miss Sinclair had always expressed her fear that her uncle would find her a match of a very low standard, almost as punishment for her father's actions."

"And so, you defended her."

"I did," Leonard muttered, brushing his fingers down his scar and seeing the way that Lord Repington's eyes flared with understanding. "There was a duel, for when I stated that I would not give Miss Sinclair to him, he demanded that I fight. Of course, I agreed to it at once, for I could not allow her to be stolen from me, not when our wedding day was growing all the nearer. Thus, my servants fetched my foil."

A groan escaped him as memories began to plunge into his heart and mind, mortifying him all over again. "I still recall looking back at the manor house and seeing the lady standing by the window. One hand was pressed against her heart, with the other lifted to me. My determination to do all I could filled me, and I turned back to my assailant." His eyes closed as he recounted the final details. "The gentleman was an excellent swordsman. The injury he gave me here was severe, but I was determined to go on. And it was then that Miss Sinclair came flying from the house, crying out for us both to stop."

"You believed she was begging for you to stop fighting with this particular gentleman so that there would be no further injury to you," Lord Repington said as Leonard nodded. "There was, I presume, the belief that she still cared for you."

Leonard's lips tugged into a rueful smile. "You have predicted the rest of the story, I see. Yes, it is as you think."

Lord Repington shook his head, his lips twisting in distaste. "Miss Sinclair went into the arms of the other gentleman."

"She did," Leonard admitted. "I later discovered that she had been writing to him earnestly, begging him to come and save her from this forced marriage that her late father had arranged. And he, of course, believing himself to be in love with her, made plans to come for her."

Silence filled the room for a long moment. Then, Lord Repington threw himself from his chair and began to march up and down the room, clearly trying to understand all that Leonard had said.

"But why would she do so?" he asked as Leonard sighed inwardly, aware that his explanations were not yet at an end. "Why would she marry another when she was quite content with you?"

"Because Lord Moore—the gentleman she *did* marry in the end—had a great deal more wealth than I," Leonard told him. "I was not the first gentleman she had sought out in this way. I believe I was the third. Beginning with a baronet, Miss Sinclair tried to do all she could to gain as much wealth as she could for herself. There was—and still is, I believe—an eagerness to live a life of freedom, without being held back by the bonds of marriage or ties to family."

Lord Repington made some indistinct noise in the back of his throat and shook his head again before picking up his brandy and throwing the rest back in one gulp.

"It was Lord Moore who came to fight me that day," Leonard said softly. "He must have had a great deal of wealth, for she allowed herself to marry him. I came to London for the Season to search for her, to demand answers from her, although, of course, she was not there."

Lord Repington's brow lifted. "That was the Season we were first acquainted."

Leonard nodded. "I put her from my mind after that, realizing that there was nothing to be done. Now, however, some years later, she has come back to London as a widow—and a poor one at that."

"Poor?" Lord Repington scoffed, swinging around to face Leonard. "How can that be so when she has accumulated so much of her own?"

A small smile tugged at Leonard's lips. "Her husband has left her with nothing," he told his friend, who stared at him in astonishment. "I want to believe that Lord Moore soon realized the truth about his wife and thus made certain that she would gain nothing upon his death.

She may live as she pleases for a while, but it will not last."

"And she will need to marry again."

"Or," Leonard said heavily, "she will need to take what I gave her so long ago—that promise, those written words that state I would give my life rather than see her struck down in poverty and loneliness again—and use it against me." His eyes lifted sadly towards his friend, who had closed his eyes tightly.

"And that is why you have brought your engagement to an end," Lord Repington said slowly. "For fear that Miss Brooks will somehow be involved in Lady Moore's schemes."

"For fear that she will be all the more embarrassed and ashamed, should she have remained as my betrothed, only to hear that another has a claim to me first," Leonard said heavily. "I do not intend to marry Lady Moore, but her demands are that either I do so, or I give her whatever she asks for, whatever she requires—just as I have promised."

"But that is ridiculous!" Lord Repington exclaimed, gesticulating furiously. "That was many years ago! She chose to wed another, did she not?"

Leonard nodded. "But that will make no difference to her. She could—as she has threatened—make the *ton* believe that she was only given such a promise recently— within, perhaps, her mourning period—and that the locket was a gift to her to make certain that she knew of my loyalty to her."

Lord Repington shook his head, then ran one hand through his hair as he blew out a long breath. "But such a thing would be manipulative indeed," he said slowly. "To claim such a thing would be to state that she has first claim over you, and that you then went on to make an arrangement with Lord Coulbourne full in the knowledge that you already intended to wed another."

Leonard hung his head as Lord Repington stated his difficulty precisely. "I shall be thrown from society and never again be able to wed. Not only that, but I shall injure Miss Brooks so deeply that I fear she might never recover." Closing his eyes tightly, he let out a pained groan. "In separating myself from her, I am doing all I can to protect her from the truth and desperate torment that would have come with our connection."

"But surely you cannot be intending to marry Lady Moore!" Lord Repington exclaimed. "You said so not a moment or two ago."

"I have no intention of going *near* Lady Moore," Leonard replied firmly. "But that does not mean that I shall not have to give in to all that she demands. Else she shall make all of the *ton* aware of the supposedly recent agreement between us—and I shall have no choice but to do so." Looking at his friend, he spread his hands. "And neither could I marry Miss Brooks full in the knowledge that I would, most likely, have Lady Moore's constant presence near to my mind and to my company for as long as she wished it. I would have had to keep her a secret, would have had to ensure that nothing was ever known of her—and that would not have been fair to Miss Brooks. It would not have been right for me to do either—but if I had wed her and then told her of it, what trouble that would have brought! What distrust would have been sown between us?" His shoulders slumped. "I had to break things off and cause her only a little pain now rather than an ongoing pain later."

Lord Repington frowned hard, squeezing his eyes shut as though he were desperate to think of some successful outcome that would ensure Leonard's happiness with Miss Brooks as well as remove Lady Moore's hands from around Leonard's throat. There was quiet for some minutes, but Leonard knew it was hopeless. There was nothing to be done. There was no easy conclusion. He had to walk this path alone.

"Then are you to return to your estate?" Lord Repington asked, looking as hopeless as Leonard now felt. "Will you leave London?"

Leonard gestured to the letters that he had set down. "Lady Moore will not allow it," he said with a harsh laugh. "She states that I am to meet with her and, if I do not, then..." Shrugging, he looked at Lord Repington. "You know very well what her threats are."

"And so you must give in to her," Lord Repington muttered, clearly upset. "But you shall not always have to do so, Stafford."

Confused, Leonard frowned. "What do you mean?"

"There must be *something* that we can do," Lord Repington said firmly. "Do you really think that, after all you have told me, that I am simply going to return to my life as it was and allow you to struggle on alone?" He smiled, and Leonard felt his spirits try to tug themselves free from the doldrums. "I shall not judge you, as you fear. I shall not mock you nor berate you. Instead, I shall work alongside you in the hope that there will be some

way for you to free yourself from Lady Moore for good."
With a grin, he picked up his brandy glass, only to realize
that it was empty. Striding across the room, he picked up
the decanter and proceeded to pour both himself and
Leonard a drink. Handing it to him, Lord Repington held
his glass aloft. "What say you, old boy?"

Leonard struggled to find the right words to express
just how grateful he was to his friend. Instead of judging
him, Lord Repington had proven his good character, and
Leonard was truly grateful for the strong friendship
between them.

"The only thing I can say is thank you," he said,
seeing a tiny spark of light in the midst of his shroud of
darkness. "And that I hope what you predict will be
true."

"Of course it will," Lord Repington replied with a
firmness in his voice that Leonard did not have himself.
"She shall not succeed, Stafford, I am sure of it. In fact, I
am determined she shall not."

"I can drink to that," Leonard replied, clinking his
glass to Lord Repington's, before finally taking a sip.

CHAPTER EIGHT

"Should you like to return home?"

Ellen looked up at her mother, her tired eyes watching her daughter carefully. Her heart ached desperately within her, for as much as she wanted to state that yes, she wanted nothing more than to leave London and make her way back to her father's estate, she knew very well that she was not able to do so.

"We cannot leave London, Mama," she said gently as Lady Newfield looked on. "Father seems to be making something of a recovery, does he not? And to move him now, to make him endure such a long journey home, would certainly not be wise."

Lady Newfield's smile was gentle and encouraging, whilst Lady Coulbourne let out a long breath of relief, making Ellen all too aware of just how much her mother was depending on her.

"I should be glad to remain in London," Ellen lied, trying to smile at her mother. "Although I think it would be best if we did not tell father what Lord Stafford has decided. Not yet, at least."

"I am in perfect agreement," Lady Newfield said quickly, turning to Lady Coulbourne. "It is a serious matter, of course, but not as serious as Lord Coulbourne's illness and his need to recover."

Lady Coulbourne nodded gently, although her eyes continued to search Ellen's face. Knowing that her mother was greatly concerned for her, Ellen tried to smile, ignoring the pain that lanced her heart as she did so. This was nothing more than a pretense, nothing more than a mask that she wore in front of her eyes so that no one could see the true depths of her pain.

"You will not need to go out into society, however, Ellen," Lady Coulbourne said gently. "I know that even the thought of such a thing is—"

"I will be quite all right, Mama," Ellen replied, ignoring the fact that even the thought of stepping out into society filled her with dread. "I shall not hide away, for that will surely only bring about more whispering and rumor from the *ton*." Instead, she smiled at her mother, who, after a moment, managed to smile back.

Lady Newfield reached across and patted Lady Coulbourne's arm. "And I shall go with your daughter whenever she wishes to go out into society, Lady Coulbourne," she said reassuringly. "You need have no doubt that I will defend her if I must."

This, Ellen had to admit, was a little comforting. Given Lady Newfield's strong resolution, Ellen was quite certain that she need not fear any sly or snide remarks being given to her directly, for Lady Newfield would not even permit them to be spoken.

"Then you have intentions of going out this afternoon?" Lady Coulbourne asked, still watching Ellen carefully. "You are aware, I am sure, that there are a few gentlemen who seek to call on you today. And a few ladies also."

Ellen's stomach tightened and she sat forward in alarm. "You have not accepted any, Mama?"

"I have not," Lady Coulbourne replied, a slight air of coldness about her now. Her eyes flashed as she looked to Lady Newfield and then back to Ellen. "I am fully aware that these visits are *not* to bring you comfort, but rather to garner whatever information they can in order to add it to the rumors that are, no doubt, already flying."

Lady Newfield clicked her tongue and sighed heavily. "The *ton* can be a cruel creature," she said, looking to Ellen. "But I would think it wise that we step out of doors for a time this afternoon, if only to make certain that we avoid anyone who might choose to call regardless of Lady Coulbourne's refusal."

Knowing that such a suggestion was wise and yet still afraid about making her way through the London streets when her shame and mortification were still so high, Ellen found it difficult to agree.

"We can take my carriage," Lady Newfield continued after a moment. "And perhaps merely take a short ride through London. There may be a quiet bookshop that we can peruse, but that is only, of course, if you feel able to do such a thing."

"Very well," Ellen agreed, thinking to herself that she

had no intention of stepping out of the carriage at all. "Thank you, Lady Newfield. That is very kind of you." Seeing the relief in her mother's expression, Ellen smiled as brightly as she could at her. "You must not concern yourself with me, Mama. I shall be quite all right, in time. Your sole responsibility is to Father. His recovery is the only thing of consequence."

"Might I ask how you are, Miss Brooks?"

Ellen sat back in the carriage seat and forced her eyes away from the window. Lady Newfield was watching her with a somewhat searching gaze, and Ellen shifted a little, feeling a trifle uncomfortable.

"You have not told your mother the truth of your emotions," Lady Newfield continued calmly. "I can see that you are in great distress, even though you hide it well." She smiled at Ellen, who felt nothing but agony beginning to swell up within her, desperate to keep all that she felt pressed down and hidden away. "I commend you for your consideration and your kindness towards your mother in doing such a thing, Miss Brooks. Your gentle heart speaks of a truly magnificent character, and I must praise you for it."

"You are very kind, Lady Newfield," Ellen began, "but there is no need to discuss my own struggles. I am in deep distress over Lord Stafford's choice, of course, but what can be done about it?" She tried to shrug, to keep her demeanor entirely nonchalant, but given the look on Lady Newfield's face, it was clearly not as believable as she had hoped. The carriage trundled on through the London streets, turning one way and then the next without any particular destination in mind. And all the while, Lady Newfield continued to watch Ellen with a gentle smile lifting the corners of her mouth, her eyes soft and her readiness to listen more than a little apparent.

And, eventually, Ellen found the words tumbling from her mouth.

"I do not know what to make of it," she said, throwing her hands up furiously. "One moment, I am deeply upset over his behavior, finding tears coming to my eyes and my heart aching. The next, I am furious!"

"You are angry," Lady Newfield said placatingly. "That is quite understandable."

Ellen shook her head. "I am not merely angry; I am filled with such a rage that it is all I can to do prevent myself from making my way to his townhouse and thundering on the door until he finally gives in to my demands and tells me the truth!"

"That must be very troubling indeed," Lady Newfield said as Ellen closed her eyes, feeling a swell of pain seal her lips closed for a few moments. "You do not know *why* Lord Stafford has done such a thing, and it does not make any particular sense, given that he has declared himself to be so contented with the match."

Much to her embarrassment, when Ellen opened her eyes, tears began to spill down her cheeks. "We cared for each other, Lady Newfield," she said, her voice broken with emotion as Lady Newfield quickly pulled out a lace handkerchief and handed it to her. "In fact, I am certain that he still does." Pressing the handkerchief to her eyes,

Ellen did her best to control herself a little more, not wanting to make a fool of herself in front of the lady. "I should not have done so, of course, but I did all I could to encourage him to stay, to continue on with our betrothal."

She did not need to explain, it seemed, for Lady Newfield nodded in a very sage manner. "And I presume that he responded to you?" she asked as Ellen nodded. "That does, indeed, make it all the more difficult to understand."

"He did not give me any reason," Ellen cried, fresh tears springing to her eyes. "I do not understand. Why should he turn his back on me when we were so close to making a contented life?"

Lady Newfield said nothing for a few moments, turning her head to look out of the carriage window instead of directly at Ellen. Fearing that she had made too big an exclamation, Ellen lapsed into silence, dropping her head and forcing the rest of her tears back. Lady Newfield had been quite correct to state that Ellen had been hiding her true feelings from everyone. Given the opportunity, it seemed now that they all burned through her at once, exploding from her as she cried until she was left with nothing but weakness.

"Might I make a suggestion, Miss Brooks?" Lady Newfield said quietly, turning back to look at Ellen. "You do not have to accept it, of course, but I should be glad to offer you the little wisdom I have."

Ellen, who had managed to stop her tears, looked up at the lady, the handkerchief now twisted between her fingers. "I should be glad of any advice, Lady Newfield," she said honestly. "To be caught up in such differing emotions and to keep the truth of my heart from my mother as well as doing all I can for my father..." She closed her eyes, pushing back her tears. "These last days have felt as though I am attempting to climb a very high mountain, but that it continually threatens to overwhelm me."

Lady Newfield smiled sadly, giving Ellen the impression that she knew all too well of what she spoke.

"Then I shall state, at the first, that you are not to battle on alone," she said firmly. "You are to talk to me whenever you wish it, knowing that I am always willing to listen to you. Secondly, however, I believe that, before you, you have a choice."

Frowning, Ellen made to ask what such a choice was, only to stop herself from saying a single word. Now was the time for her to listen.

"You are upset and angry with Lord Stafford's decision," Lady Newfield continued, waving a hand. "I can well understand it. It does not make sense, particularly when it appears that you both were beginning to care deeply for each other." She smiled at Ellen, who could only nod, unable to find the voice she needed to agree. "He obviously wanted to remain betrothed, given what you have said," Lady Newfield continued a little more gently. "And yet, he cried off regardless."

Ellen closed her eyes. "He said he had no choice," she said, her voice nothing more than a whisper. "There was nothing he could do."

"Then the choice is still clear to you," Lady Newfield replied practically. "You must decide whether or not you are willing to accept such a statement from him."

A little confused, Ellen opened her eyes and studied Lady Newfield, who was still smiling. "I do not know what you mean," she said slowly. "There is *nothing* I can do. Our betrothal is at an end. He has decided it; he has cried off. I have written to him every day, begging him to speak, but he does not return my letters. I must give up, I think. What else can be done?"

"Ah, but that is where you are quite mistaken," Lady Newfield replied with a broad smile, one finger shaking gently in Ellen's direction. "The day I set foot in this house, I knew all too well that you were not a lady to be easily trifled with. Your mother has spoken to me of your stubborn nature—but do not think that I am here to criticize such a thing! Rather, I am here to tell you that such a characteristic might become very useful indeed."

This did not seem particularly likely to Ellen, given that she had been constantly berated by both her mother and her father for many years on such a subject.

"I can see you do not believe me," Lady Newfield said, laughing. "But as I said, there is a choice before you, and you must decide what you are to do. Either, Miss Brooks, you accept the situation as it stands and, in doing so, shall never know why Lord Stafford did such a thing and shall be separated from him for good."

"Or?" Ellen asked, her heart seeming to squeeze with a sudden flurry of hope.

"Or," Lady Newfield replied, her eyes gleaming, "you harness that determined spirit that is within you and you do *not* give up. Instead, you find a strength within yourself to seek out Lord Stafford, and, in whatever way you can, you do all you must to find out the truth, knowing that, in doing so, there is still a sliver of hope that all might come aright."

It was as though Lady Newfield had struck her with a hammer blow, for Ellen felt herself shudder violently, her hands tightening together as she clasped them hard in her lap. She had never even *thought* of such a thing, having resigned herself to the fact that she would have to endure this situation.

"I should warn you, however," Lady Newfield said, reaching across and touching Ellen's hand, startling her into alertness again. "Should you choose to take the second path and decide that you must chase the truth, then there may very well be consequences for you within that."

"Consequences?" Ellen asked faintly. "What do you mean?"

Lady Newfield's expression was severe. "It may be that the gentleman is hiding his true purpose in ending the betrothal in order to protect you, Miss Brooks," she said gently. "You may find yourself fully aware of all that has taken place and yet in such deep distress that you will turn your back on him anyway."

Considering this, Ellen took in a few long breaths before finally allowing herself to nod slowly. It was as though Lady Newfield had shone a new light into her dark life, had revealed to her a secret passage that Ellen had never even known was there. Her words had awoken something within Ellen that she wanted to cling to, something that she wanted to hold onto tightly again. That stubbornness that her mother had so often cried over was now, she realized, something that she could take hold of in this present circumstance.

"I think," she said softly, "that I should like to know the truth, no matter what I may face in the process of discovering it," she said as a glimmer of a smile appeared on Lady Newfield's face. "If I do not, I fear that I shall always be tormented by the questions that now linger in my mind, the struggle that so often seems to pull me down into despair."

Lady Newfield pressed her hand for a moment and then sat back in her chair, letting out a long and contented sigh.

"I am very glad to hear you say so," she said with a smile. "I truly believe it will bring you a little more relief than you have at present, Miss Brooks. And if you wish it, I shall be very happy to aid you."

Ellen let out a quiet laugh. "I do not think that I shall be able to do any of this without some guidance, Lady Newfield," she replied, feeling a little happier than she had for some time. "For all I have done thus far is write letters to him and wait, desperately, for a reply."

"There shall be no more of that!" Lady Newfield replied with a laugh. "No, the time has come for you to be a good deal more direct, Miss Brooks. You must speak openly to Lord Stafford in a calm, decisive manner and ensure that he is fully aware that you shall not settle for this lack of explanation."

Drawing in a long breath to steady herself, Ellen lifted her chin just a notch. "And how shall I do that?"

Lady Newfield smiled. "By being brave and bold,

Miss Brooks. Tonight, we must attend Lord Whitfield's ball."

~

DESPITE HER COURAGE earlier that day, when she had been sitting in the carriage with Lady Newfield, setting foot into Lord Whitfield's townhouse and feeling almost every eye turn towards her at once sent such a shudder of regret through Ellen that, had it not been for the comforting presence of Lady Newfield beside her, she would have turned aside at once.

"Miss Brooks!" her host exclaimed, greeting her with such a loud voice that Ellen was certain that everyone was aware of her arrival if they had not been before. "You arrive at last. And with Lady Newfield!"

"I am, of course, a willing chaperone given Lord Coulbourne's illness and Lady Coulbourne's eagerness to stay by his side," Lady Newfield replied quickly grasping Lord Whitfield's attention. "You are very kind to have extended me an invitation. This ball will be, I am sure, quite marvelous."

This seemed to distract Lord Whitfield entirely, for he quickly began to delight at having Lady Newfield present and Ellen was able to escape from their host and make her way further into the ballroom.

"You must ignore all the looks and the whispers," Lady Newfield said firmly, her arm through Ellen's already. "If gentlemen wish to dance with you, then I would suggest that you do so, though make certain to say very little."

"I do not wish to dance with anyone," Ellen replied, but Lady Newfield shook her head.

"You must," she stated unequivocally. "If you do not, then it shall only add to the rumors. They will say that you are heartbroken, that you are completely undone by such a thing. People will remark on your complexion, on your very state of being, with no positive remark being made whatsoever. However," she continued, as Ellen tried to listen carefully without thinking too much about Lord Stafford, "if you continue as you have always done, greeting acquaintances, dancing and the like, then you shall be spared some of those remarks."

Seeing the sense in Lady Newfield's words, Ellen forced herself to smile and to agree, even though she did not want to set foot onto the dance floor. Telling herself that Lady Newfield was to be her guide in this matter and that it was best, therefore, to do as she was asked, Ellen continued to meander through the ballroom, smiling and nodding to some acquaintances. When gentlemen came to her to ask her for a dance, she gave them her dance card without a modicum of hesitation. And through it all, she let her eyes search the ballroom for any sign of Lord Stafford.

"There he is."

Lady Newfield's words sent both a chill of fear and a flood of hope into Ellen's heart. She did not react immediately, however, forcing herself to behave normally as she turned slowly to stand with Lady Newfield so that she might see what she did.

It did not take long to find him. It was as if her eyes knew precisely where to look, precisely where he would be. He was standing next to another gentleman—his friend, Lord Repington, if she remembered correctly. His gaze roved over the crowd, drawing closer to her, ever closer, until Ellen could barely stand the anticipation that welled up within her.

"Smile," she heard Lady Newfield say and found her lips curving immediately.

And then, he saw her.

His expression changed at once. No longer was he the bored, dull gentleman who had stood there a moment before. Instead, his face heightened in color, his eyes widened, and his mouth fell a little ajar. Lord Repington nudged him, clearly a little confused, only to look in her direction also.

It was clear neither of them had expected to see her.

"Now we approach," Lady Newfield said quietly. "He is near to the back of the room, Miss Brooks, and you must make certain to speak to him in the shadows."

"What should I say?" Ellen asked breathlessly, her heart hammering furiously as Lord Stafford continued to watch her. "What should I tell him?"

Lady Newfield laughed softly and took her arm again. "State, quite plainly, that you shall not rest until you discover the truth. And make certain that you are entirely clear about your determination to do so. When you are finished, then turn yourself to the side and make your way from him. Do not allow him to speak or to call you back. You have told him your intention, and that is all, for the moment, that he needs to hear."

Her stomach was roiling, but Ellen lifted her head and began to walk determinedly towards Lord Stafford.

She could see his eyes widen, was fully aware of the astonishment in his expression, but forced herself to remain steadfast in her approach. She would not let him see the pain in her heart, the confusion that still clouded around her. Instead, she would make certain he understood just how tenacious she could be.

The next step, it seemed, would be entirely up to him.

CHAPTER NINE

S *he is coming this way.*

Leonard did not know what to make of this. He had not expected Miss Brooks to be present this evening and certainly had never even *thought* that she would come near to him!

"Goodness," he heard Lord Repington say, although his voice seemed faint and far away. "It seems that Miss Brooks is not quite prepared to step away from you, in the way that you are with her."

Leonard tried to speak but found his lips fastened together. His lungs began to burn, and he realized he had been holding his breath. Everything in him wanted to run to her, to catch her hands in his and to beg her forgiveness, but the knowledge that not only was Lady Moore present but, most certainly that she was probably watching him, made him all the more wary.

"Lord Stafford."

He swallowed hard, his voice rasping as he spoke. "Good evening, Miss Brooks."

She was paler than he remembered her, although her eyes were just as dazzling as before. When she spoke, however, there was a certain hardness to her voice, and her entire frame seemed fixed and steady, as though she wanted to make quite certain that nothing he said or did could injure her again.

"I—I did not expect to see you here this evening," he found himself saying, not quite sure why he was stating such a thing. "I myself have no desire to be present."

"And yet, here you are," Miss Brooks replied, walking past him towards the back of the ballroom—and Leonard found his feet following without even thinking about what he was doing or why. "I am glad to have found you, however." She turned to him, her face half-hidden in shadow. "You have not replied to my letters."

Leonard turned helplessly to Lord Repington, only to see that he had been pulled aside by Lady Newfield, who stood a few steps away from both himself and Miss Brooks, effectively shielding them from view.

"But that does not matter," Miss Brooks said with evident determination. "For I have come to inform you, Lord Stafford, that I will not simply accept what you have thrown at me. I will not merely stand aside and allow this circumstance to take hold of me."

Blinking rapidly, Leonard tried to find something to say but instead found himself shaking his head.

"No doubt you will try to dissuade me," Miss Brooks continued with a slightly scornful look in her eyes. "But I am quite determined, Lord Stafford. I will not be pushed aside. I *will* discover the truth."

"The truth?" he croaked, a great and terrible fear catching him. "What do you mean?"

Miss Brooks looked at him steadily, her gaze not flickering for even a moment. "I mean that I shall find out the reasons behind the ending of our betrothal," she told him plainly. "You are determined not to permit me to know, but that shall not deter me. Whether you wish to be of assistance to me or not in this matter, I assure you that I shall not rest until I finally know all."

Leonard's whole body trembled violently for a moment—something he was certain Miss Brooks noticed. He tried to find something to say, something to turn her aside from this particular course of action, but nothing came to his lips. All he could feel was terror, his mind blank with fear. If she discovered the truth, then all that he had been trying to protect her from would burn up in smoke. What was he to do? Volunteer such information when he wanted nothing more than to hide it from her?

"If you wish to speak to me about this matter further, then I am sure you will be able to find me," Miss Brooks finished when he said nothing. Her tone was cool, matter of fact, and still, Leonard could find nothing to say. "Whilst it appears that *you* are willing to set aside the happiness that was within arm's reach of us both, I can assure you that I, Lord Stafford, am not." With a quick curtsy, she gave him a tight smile, lifted her chin, and turned away.

Leonard could barely breathe. He stared after her, desperate to find something to say, something that would make her aware of his need to remain at arm's length from her, his desire to protect her—but his lips would not move, his voice refusing to make a single sound. Miss Brooks approached Lady Newfield, greeted Lord Repington quickly, and then together, the two ladies made their way back across the ballroom.

Leonard did not miss how so many looks and quick glances followed after her—and found himself all the more ashamed. He was the one who had brought this shame upon her, he knew, but still, the choice to do otherwise remained firmly closed to him.

"Whatever did Miss Brooks want to say?"

Jerking violently at the sound of Lord Repington's voice, having not realized that his friend was so near, Leonard forced his gaze away from Miss Brooks and looked up blankly at his friend.

"Whatever it was, it has clearly alarmed you," Lord Repington continued with evident concern. "Pray tell me that her words were not solely to injure you! I did not think that she had such a character."

Feverishly, Leonard shook his head. He did not want Lord Repington to think badly of Miss Brooks.

"She—she is determined that she shall not let the matter rest," he breathed, finding himself still too overcome to speak with any great force. "The words she spoke tore at my heart, for she is quite resolute in her intentions."

Lord Repington's brow rose. "You mean to say that she will seek out the truth about why you cried off?" he asked, as Leonard nodded. "My goodness, that lady is certainly tenacious!" There was a note of admiration in his voice, but Leonard could not feel any such thing. Instead, there was only deep, unsettling anxiety and awareness that Miss Brooks would do *precisely* as she intended. He knew her well enough to know that her words were not spoken lightly.

"And now it seems your troubles are to multiply," Lord Repington muttered, elbowing Leonard hard in the ribs. "It appears that Lady Moore has been watching you and your conversation with Miss Brooks. Look, she is approaching."

Leonard stiffened. "You need not depart," Leonard replied quickly. "It will be good for her to know that I have not kept my secrets entirely to myself."

Lord Repington chuckled darkly, his eyes flicking towards Lady Moore and then returning to Leonard. "I have no intention of going anywhere, Stafford," he said, his tone light but his expression becoming a little angry. "I should *very* much like it if Lady Moore becomes aware that I know all about her little scheme."

Grateful for Lord Repington's support, Leonard cleared his throat and tried to mentally prepare himself for what Lady Moore would say next. They had not spoken since the evening assembly and he had refused to reply to any of her letters—although such a thing had been, perhaps, a little foolish, given all that was at stake.

"Lord Stafford."

He glanced at her but did not bow, feeling himself stiffening instead. "Lady Moore."

"And I see you have your friend with you this evening," Lady Moore purred, looking towards Lord Repington, who only arched a brow. "It appears you have spoken to him at length, Lord Stafford."

"I have," Leonard replied tightly. "What is it you

wish to speak to me about, Lady Moore?" He eyed her sharply, aware of just how beautiful she was but feeling nothing but anger and despair in her company. "I have no desire to remain here by your side for any great length of time."

This seemed to shock Lady Moore into silence, for her eyes rounded as she looked back at him, as though she had been expecting him to fall at her feet instead.

"You are a little rude, Lord Stafford," she replied in an injured tone. "Why, I thought you should be glad of my company, given the pain you must be in at present."

Leonard bit the inside of his cheeks to keep from retorting. Most likely, Lady Moore had discovered his engagement to Miss Brooks and now knew that he had cried off. No doubt she took great pleasure in his trouble, feeling herself proud that she had managed to do such a thing simply by returning to London.

"You will not speak to me of Miss Brooks, then?" she asked, as Leonard turned his eyes away from her, seeing Lord Repington's dark frown and angry expression. "What a shame. She appears to be such a lovely young lady."

"Leave her be!" Leonard exclaimed, rounding on Lady Moore, who took a small step back. "I have cried off simply to protect her from not only my foolish past, but also from you, Lady Moore. You will not go near her." It was a hollow threat given that he had nothing to intimidate Lady Moore with, nothing that he could put to her that would force her to comply, but the words were forceful in their own right.

Lady Moore smiled, her eyes narrowing just a little, and Leonard felt his stomach turn over.

"You care for her," Lady Moore murmured, reaching out to put one hand on Leonard's arm, but he jerked back, avoiding her completely. "Ah, what a shame. And now, here I am, come back to London to ruin all of your carefully laid plans." Her eyes swung to Lord Repington. "I am sure that he has told you everything about me, Lord Repington, since you are glaring at me like that, but let me assure you that I care not one jot about your consideration."

Lord Repington let out a hard laugh. "I should not think that a creature such as you—that is, one with no conscience and a heart entirely absent of kindness— should give *any* consideration to what I might think, Lady Moore."

His words were cold, and Leonard felt the chill of them brush over his skin. To his satisfaction, he saw the self-satisfied smile on Lady Moore's face fade away, her eyes narrowing as she looked back towards Leonard.

"You have not replied to any of my letters."

Her words were harsh now, her voice devoid of any blithe emotion as there had been only moments before.

"No," Leonard agreed. "I have not."

"Then I shall take this opportunity to remind you, Lord Stafford, that there are consequences that are, at present, being laid out before you." She took a step closer, and Leonard fought the urge to move away, looking down at her and feeling nothing but anger burn within him. Lady Moore was just as he remembered her. Her dark hair pulled back from her delicate features, her green eyes searching his. Her lips were full, her frame small and elegant—and yet Leonard knew all too well that great cruelty was snarled up within her. There was no beauty here, no goodness. Instead, there was only a pervasive darkness that threatened once more to pull him in.

"If you do not answer me within the next day, then I shall have no choice but to speak to some within society about the *friendship* that once was between us," Lady Moore continued. "I shall begin with Miss Brooks, given that she is evidently so dear to you. Perhaps in speaking to her, I shall be able to remove all thought of your good nature from her, so that she will know the truth of your character."

"That is enough."

Lord Repington had gone a deep shade of red as he stepped closer, putting one hand on Lady Moore's arm for just a moment.

"Your words are nothing more than poison," Lord Repington continued harshly. "Remove yourself from our company at once. There is nothing more that you need say."

Leonard's heart was beating with such furiousness that it took him a moment or two to catch his breath. Lady Moore's threats were so very real that it made his heart scream aloud in terror at the thought of it.

"I—I shall reply," he said hoarsely, just as Lady Moore opened her mouth to retort something back to Lord Repington. "But I shall not wed you. I shall never permit myself to do such a thing." He drew himself up, his jaw working furiously as he looked down into her eyes. "Even the thought repulses me."

For a moment, Leonard was sure he saw a flicker of hurt in Lady Moore's eyes—but it was gone in an instant. Instead, she merely laughed, brushing off Lord Repington's hand and looking up at Leonard with what appeared to be a triumphant smile.

"I would much prefer to have my freedom, Lord Stafford," she told him, touching his hand for just a moment, making Leonard recoil physically. "I look forward to your first...*gift*...to me. I am, you see, in a little trouble with some debts that I have accrued." She tilted her head and studied him, as though wondering what the first thing would be to ask for. "I do not like being in such debts, although it has been entirely necessary to ensure that I was able to come to London!"

Leonard closed his eyes. "You want me to pay your debts for you."

"Indeed," Lady Moore replied with a shrug of her delicate shoulders. "That should not be too much trouble, I think." She laughed again, her eyes dancing and a bright smile on her face that made Leonard want to turn away at once. "And," Lady Moore continued, her tone a little less mischievous now, "it would prove to me that your intentions are genuine, Lord Stafford. Although I can hardly expect you to refuse, given what is at stake!"

Words of anger burned Leonard's throat, but he held them back, forcing his teeth together, his lips to remain closed. To speak to her now in such a fashion would only do more harm than good. As much as he disliked being her pawn, there was nothing he could do—at least for the present. He had to hope that, somehow, he and Lord

Repington could find a way to extract himself from the lady for good.

"I shall leave you now," Lady Moore said with a heavy sigh tearing from her as though she was deeply distraught at the thought of being pushed from his company. "I will, of course, write to you the morrow, Lord Stafford. Have no doubt about that."

A long, heavy breath left Leonard as he watched Lady Moore step away. There was relief in her absence, certainly, but it was not a relief that brought him any real pleasure. All there was now was the gnawing agony that came with being at her disposal.

"Goodness, she is a deeply dislikeable woman," Lord Repington muttered, shaking his head. "She bears no sense of guilt or shame over what she is doing."

"No," Leonard agreed heavily. "She does not—and I have no choice but to do as she asks." He lifted his gaze to follow after Lady Moore, feeling that tight band across his chest as he wondered who she was to speak to next and fearing that it would be about matters to do with them both. His heart twisted furiously as he saw her making her way directly towards Miss Brooks, who had only just finished dancing with a gentleman he did not recognize.

"Good heavens, no!" he breathed, as Lord Repington looked quickly in the very same direction. "How can she..."

Lord Repington let out a guttural sound that spoke entirely of the deep dislike he now held for Lady Moore.

"She is doing so simply to torment you," Lord

Repington said in what Leonard supposed was meant to be a reassuring tone. "It is a warning, of sorts."

"A warning?" Leonard gasped, hardly able to get air into his lungs. "Lady Moore has deliberately gone to make introductions to Lady Newfield and Miss Brooks!"

Lord Repington moved and came to stand directly in front of Leonard, cutting off his view. He made to protest, to step aside so that he might continue to watch, but Lord Repington held out a hand.

"Lady Moore is doing all she can to torment you," he said as Leonard tried to get his breathing under control. "In making certain that she is introduced to Miss Brooks and to Lady Newfield, she is reminding you that she has great power in this situation. That is all. Do not allow her to see you staring after her, for no doubt, she will glance towards us in a moment in the hope that you will be doing precisely that. It will bring her nothing but satisfaction."

Still, Leonard struggled to draw in air, wanting desperately to push Lord Repington aside, but at the same time, trying to allow his friend's words to penetrate his mind. Lord Repington remained steadfast, refusing to move aside but watching Leonard carefully as though he feared he might deliberately force him to do so.

"She has great power over me," Leonard muttered, pushing one hand through his hair and turning aside so that he could no longer see Lady Moore. In fact, he moved all the more so that he had his back to the lady, seeing the wisdom in what Lord Repington had said. "I cannot see any way out at present."

"We will think of something," Lord Repington

replied with more confidence than Leonard himself had. "But the question for the moment must be what you are to do about Miss Brooks."

Leonard groaned aloud and shook his head. "I do not know!" he exclaimed, throwing up his hands. "Whatever I do, I am afraid of the consequences that will follow. If I say nothing, I am certain that she will discover the truth on her own—albeit after some time. If I tell her now, then she will be horrified with me, turning aside from me without hesitation."

Lord Repington tilted his head, his eyes drifting away as he considered. "I think that you give Miss Brooks no particular credit," he said mildly, surprising Leonard. "What if she does not react as you expect?"

"What if she does?" Leonard retorted, throwing up his hands. "It is not a risk I am willing to take at present."

With a small sigh, Lord Repington spread his hands. "Then in making such a choice, you leave her to find out the truth alone, and, in doing so, she might think all the worse of you for refusing to tell her of your own accord," he said, making Leonard's heart quicken for a moment. "Would it not be best to tell her all, given that she is so determined and, therefore, certain to find out the truth regardless of how well you have tried to hide it, tried to protect her from it?"

Leonard shook his head, his thoughts beginning to come at him with such speed, with such force, that it was hard indeed to think at all clearly.

"These are matters you *must* consider," Lord Repington finished as the music for the next dance began to swell around them. "Choose wisely, friend. It may be that one path will only bring you more pain, whilst the other..."

Looking up, Leonard waited expectantly for Lord Repington to finish, not quite certain what he was to say.

"Whilst the other," Lord Repington murmured, his eyes now fixed on someone behind Leonard, someone that Leonard just knew to be Miss Brooks. "The other path, Lord Stafford, might bring you more happiness than you can, at present, imagine. You must only take a chance."

CHAPTER TEN

Ellen rose from her father's bedside and, leaning forward, kissed his brow. A small smile lingered on her face as she made her way towards the door. In spite of all her troubles, in spite of her difficulties, it appeared that her father was continuing his recovery, albeit slowly. His speech was no longer as slurred—although that might be, she considered, because she was beginning to find it easier to understand him. Though his grip on her hand was certainly stronger, and he could now move his toes, which was something of a wonder.

She sighed contentedly and made her way back to her own bedchamber, ready to have Betty ensure she was quite prepared for afternoon calls.

"Good afternoon, my lady."

Betty was ready and smiling, greeting Ellen with a bobbed curtsy.

"And how is the master this afternoon?"

"He is improving," Ellen said, finding the words

bringing her a good deal of comfort. "It will be a long time yet, but I am hopeful."

Pressing one hand to her heart, Betty let out a sigh of relief. "I am very glad to hear it, my lady."

Ellen pressed her lips together and then spoke again, fearing that the answer she was about to hear would be the same as all the other times. "You took the letter to Lord Stafford?"

Much to her surprise, a slight blush caught Betty's cheeks, although she quickly dipped her head as though to hide it. "I did, my lady."

"And was there a reply?"

Betty's eyes lifted, and she gave a sad shake of her head. "One of the household staff asked me to wait for a few minutes, but there was nothing immediate," she said, clearly aware that this injured Ellen a little. "I am sure that, in time—"

"The person who asked you to linger," Ellen interrupted, forcing herself not to think about Lord Stafford but instead to speak to Betty about the reason for her blush. Perhaps it would take her mind from her own troubles at present! "Was he the same fellow that brings—or, at the very least—used to bring notes from Lord Stafford?"

From the way that Betty's eyes rounded and her mouth opened without a single sound coming from it gave Ellen her answer. She could not help but smile, as Betty flushed a deep crimson and dropped her head.

"I must hope then, for both our sakes, that Lord Stafford is inclined towards writing to me this afternoon," she said, laughing as she sat down in front of the dressing table. "I do hope he is a good sort of person, Betty."

Her maid said nothing, her cheeks still a very bright red and her fingers trembling just a little as she checked Ellen's tresses. Ellen could not help but laugh again and, after a moment, Betty joined in also.

"If anyone is to be happy, Betty, then I must hope you shall be," Ellen said with a heavy sigh. "I do not think there is even the smallest chance that Lord Stafford will change his mind."

"There is always a chance, my lady," came Betty's reply. "Lady Coventry was in the most dreadful of situations before she came to London, and now look how contented she is." Her smile was warm as she thought of her previous mistress. "There is always a little bit of hope, my lady, even when you believe there is nothing there at all."

Ellen let out a long breath and looked back at her reflection in the mirror. After yesterday evening's ball, she had hoped that Lord Stafford would come to his senses and determine that yes, he would speak to her about all that was going on since she was set on finding it out regardless—but he had not come near to her again for the rest of the evening. Lady Newfield had then instructed her to write to him the following afternoon, reminding him of what had been said and nothing more— and thus, Ellen had done so. So far, however, it seemed that Lord Stafford was not to be moved. He appeared to be just as determined as before, although, she considered, perhaps she was not giving him a good deal of time to alter his thinking.

"A little hope," she whispered, as Betty finished pinning up one or two loose curls. "That is all I need cling to. A *little* hope."

"Yes, my lady," Betty answered, stepping back as Ellen rose to her feet. "That is all you need to have."

∽

"WHERE ARE we to go this afternoon?"

Lady Newfield arched one eyebrow at her. "Can you not think?"

Ellen's mouth fell open, and she had to quickly regain her composure so that she would not look improper.

"Of *course* we are to go to speak to Lord Stafford," Lady Newfield answered with a wave of her hand. "It is of the greatest importance. All you are to do is to reiterate what you have said before." Her brows lowered, and she looked at Ellen askance. "And you are to make mention of one more thing."

Ellen looked back at her. "Oh?"

"Tell me," Lady Newfield said, after a moment or two, "did you notice anything a little strange last evening, once we finished speaking to Lord Stafford?"

Casting her mind back, Ellen found herself recalling only the emotions she had struggled to deal with rather than any particular person. Once she had finished conversing with Lord Stafford, she and Lady Newfield had gone away from Lord Stafford and Lord Repington, but Ellen had not had any sense of joy or gladness in her heart. Rather, there had been a dull ache in her chest that spoke of only frustration and sorrow. She had spent the next few minutes in something of a daze, only to be tugged away into a dance by Lord Castleton.

"I—I do not precisely recall," she said honestly, feeling a little embarrassed that there was evidently something she had not seen that she ought to have. "What did you notice, Lady Newfield?"

Lady Newfield leaned forward. "When you departed from Lord Stafford's side, there quickly came another lady to speak to him. They spoke at length, and from what I observed, it did not appear as though he was glad to have her in his company."

Thinking to herself that she did not understand the significance of such a remark, Ellen waited patiently for Lady Newfield to continue. The lady smiled at her, although there was a flicker of anger in her eyes.

"That very same lady, once she had finished speaking to Lord Stafford, then came near to us," she explained. "She used the acquaintance of Lord Castleton to seek an introduction to us both and then spoke for some minutes thereafter."

Ellen frowned. "You mean to say that Lady Moore was speaking to Lord Stafford first?" she said, recalling how she had been introduced to the lady by Lord Castleton. She had thought the lady very charming indeed, with a kind manner and gentle smile. "I do not see why such a thing should be of interest."

Lady Newfield shrugged. "It may not be important in the least," she said, looking out of the carriage window to see how close they were now to Lord Stafford's townhouse. "But I did notice that she glanced behind her on two occasions, as though eager to seek Lord Stafford's attention. Therefore, I think you should speak to Lord Stafford and mention Lady Moore's name to him." Looking back at Ellen with a small smile, her eyes twinkling, she spread her hands. "What harm can it do?"

Thinking quickly, Ellen considered what had been said. "You mean that you wish me to see the reaction that such a name gives him," she said, feeling her stomach dropping as a sense of dread swamped her. "Do you think that he has chosen her over me?"

Lady Newfield's eyes flared wide in an instant. "No, good gracious, no!" she exclaimed, making Ellen's despair lift for just a moment. "I do not think that at all. Rather," she continued, as the carriage began to slow, "I believe that whilst this situation has something to do with Lady Moore, it may be due to an entirely different circumstance than what you think."

Given that she could not think of any other circumstance aside from this one, Ellen had to trust that Lady Newfield had other suggestions in mind. Her stomach began to twist and turn as she climbed out of the carriage, her nerves rising, unbidden, up through her.

Her breathing quickened as Lady Newfield took her arm and walked up the steps towards the front door. It was opened before they arrived, with the butler bowing graciously as Lady Newfield handed him both their cards.

"Please inform your master that we have every intention of seeing him today and that it is most urgent," Lady Newfield said briskly as they were shown inside. "It is vital that we speak to him."

The butler promised to do so and then made his way

a little further into the house. Ellen stood waiting patiently, her mind filled with all manner of thoughts, including whether or not Lord Stafford was, in fact, interested in any way in Lady Moore. After all, the lady had a startling beauty while she herself, Ellen knew, bore no particular loveliness. Lord Stafford had complimented her a good many times, for which she was grateful, but still, it felt as though there was a very significant gap between herself and Lady Moore. She could hardly blame him for his interest in the lady, should it be proven.

"The butler is taking a while," Lady Newfield remarked as there came a quiet rap at the door, which, much to Ellen's surprise, was then pushed open. Lord Repington appeared, walking into the house as though it was just as much his own as Lord Stafford's.

"Good afternoon, Miss Brooks, Lady Newfield!" he exclaimed, smiling broadly at them both as he walked into the house before stopping to bow. "Are you come to call upon Lord Stafford?"

Ellen, who found herself liking this particular gentleman, gave him a small smile. "We are waiting to see whether or not we shall be permitted entry, Lord Repington."

Snorting, Lord Repington waved a hand. "Nonsense," he said with a gesture for them both to follow. "Whether Lord Stafford wishes to see you or not, I think that he ought to do so—out of sheer politeness if nothing else!"

Lady Newfield glanced at Ellen before nodding, encouraging her to follow after Lord Repington. Just as they did so, the butler reappeared, looking flustered that he had taken so long.

"Lady Newfield," he said, inclining his head quickly, "I am sorry to inform you but Lord Stafford is quite unable to see you at present. He is expecting a visitor."

Lord Repington laughed and clapped the butler on the back, making the man stumble forward slightly.

"He is only expecting me, and I am here and quite content for both these ladies to join us," he said as the butler began to stammer, caught between doing as his master had asked and what Lord Repington had said. "Make sure there are enough refreshments sent for us all." With a smile, he beckoned to Ellen and Lady Newfield and continued walking, clearly quite sure of himself.

"You are a good friend of Lord Stafford's, I think," Ellen said quietly as Lord Repington laughed.

"We are almost as close as brothers might be," Lord Repington replied with satisfaction. "I can assure you, Miss Brooks, that you will be welcomed into Lord Stafford's house, even if he is doing all he can to remove you from his presence!"

Ellen came to a sudden stop, making Lord Repington turn to look at her. "If you are as close as brothers, Lord Repington, then you must know why he continues to push me away and why he has brought our engagement to an end." It was a bold statement, she knew, but it was as Lady Newfield had said. She needed to find her determination and tenacity again if she were ever to discover what was going on.

The smile disappeared from Lord Repington's face at once, and he turned so that he might face her a little more fully.

"There is loyalty between two brothers, be they kin or not," he said a little sternly. "It is not my position to explain all to you, Miss Brooks, and thus, I shall not do so. However," he continued as a flush of embarrassment began to creep into Ellen's cheeks, "what I will say is that he is doing all he can to protect you, Miss Brooks." A muscle twitched in his cheek, and a glimmer of a smile reappeared. "And I, as his friend, am doing all I can to protect him—which is why I am bringing you in to see him, Miss Brooks. Lord Stafford may be completely decided in this situation, but I can assure you that I am not!"

Ellen nodded, a sense that she had been almost reprimanded by Lord Repington creeping in about her, but a quick smile from Lady Newfield reassured her.

"This way," Lord Repington continued, leading them further into the house. "No doubt, he will be in the library or the study at this time of the morning." He threw Ellen a quick smile, reassuring her more. "He likes to read or study particular matters of business in the early afternoon, before taking calls and the like."

Ellen's breathing was quick and fast as Lord Repington stepped boldly into the library before exclaiming loudly to Lord Stafford, who was evidently inside. One hand pressed to her stomach as she made her way in after him, feeling almost sick with nerves. Would Lord Stafford refuse to see her? Would he remain silent, choosing to speak to anyone but her? Her eyes searched the room as she came in after Lord Repington, finally discovering Lord Stafford sitting in the corner of the room, a book in one hand and a glass of something in the other.

The shock on his face was undeniable as he caught sight of both her and Lady Newfield. With a stammered apology, he rose to his feet, setting first the books and then the brandy down, bowing hastily and then gesturing for them both to sit down.

"The butler said you were waiting for someone to call, but I told him that I did not mind if Lady Newfield and Miss Brooks were present also," Lord Repington said easily, gaining him a dark look from Lord Stafford. "You do not mind, I am sure."

Before he could reply, Ellen gathered her courage about her and spoke directly to Lord Stafford.

"I am here to speak to you about Lady Moore, Lord Stafford."

Her eyes pinned to his face, she studied each change that came upon it. Lady Newfield had been quite correct, it seemed, for he paled significantly, his eyes widened just a touch. Whilst he cleared his throat and dropped his gaze, Ellen was sure that the lady meant more to him than he wanted to admit.

Her heart twisted painfully, and she forced herself to continue to study him, praying desperately that she was not about to be made a fool of.

"I know Lady Moore, certainly," Lord Stafford said. "But she is nothing of significance to me, I can assure you."

Ellen dared a glance at Lord Repington, surprised to

see the way he rolled his eyes so significantly. Evidently, Lord Stafford was not speaking the truth.

"I think she is a significant person in your life at present, Lord Stafford," she said, forcing her voice to remain steady by twining her fingers together and squeezing them tightly. "She *did* come to speak to us both last evening. I do not know if you are aware of this, but she came specifically to seek an introduction and, thereafter, to speak to us about a particular matter."

This, of course, was an untruth, for Lady Moore had spoken about very general matters and had not raised anything particular at all. Lord Stafford, however, jerked upright in his seat and stared at her with wide, furious eyes, his skin now milk white.

"What did she tell you?" he asked, his voice hoarse. "Whatever it was, I beg of you not to believe it!" Staring at her for some moments, his green eyes wide, Lord Stafford said nothing more but slowly began to sink back into his chair. His gaze dropped to his knees, and he lowered his head as though realizing just what he had said and why it was of such significance.

"Lord Stafford," Lady Newfield began, only to be interrupted by a scratch at the door. The maid entered with a tray, followed by another with a second. There were some minutes of silence while the maids set things out, giving Ellen the chance to further study Lord Stafford.

There were, by now, spots of color on his cheeks, although she could see how sweat had begun to bead on his brow. His eyes were shifting from the floor to her feet and then back again, as if he were too afraid to lift his gaze and look at her directly. There was a sense of angst coming from him, a tightness to his frame that betrayed great anxiety. What was he so afraid of? Was it that there was a relationship between himself and Lady Moore that had been brought back to life?

"Lord Stafford," Lady Newfield said again the moment the door had closed. "There is, before you, a choice." She smiled at Ellen, who could only manage a small smile in return, recalling how such a statement had been said to her also.

"A choice?" he repeated dully, although he did not lift his head. "And what is that?"

Lady Newfield spread her hands. "You can either choose to remain in silence, leaving Miss Brooks to continue searching for answers herself, or you can choose to be honest with her, allowing her to know the truth of your decision."

"If you choose not to speak," Ellen added, the idea only just coming to her, "then I shall, instead, go to Lady Moore. She will, I am certain, be more than willing to tell me everything, should I ask."

"No!" Lord Stafford seemed to explode from his chair. He flung himself to his feet, one hand stretched out towards her as though he intended to pull her from the idea with physical force. Ellen, Lady Newfield, and Lord Repington said nothing, staring at Lord Stafford in stunned silence. Eventually, Lord Stafford sank back into his chair, lowering his head into his hands.

"I do not want to speak to you of this, Miss Brooks,"

he said, his voice muffled by his hands. "I am afraid that if I do so, then you shall never wish to be in my company again."

"I can assure you, I shall listen without judgment," Ellen said, seeing Lord Repington's smile but being entirely unaware as to why she was being bestowed such a thing. "Surely you know me well enough to understand that I shall not simply throw you aside without good reason—just as I am sure that you brought our engagement to an end for a very good reason indeed." She saw him drop his hands and felt her heart surge with a sudden and desperate hope. "You are trying to protect me, are you not?"

Lord Stafford lifted his head, and there was such a look of agony on his face that Ellen wanted to go to him at once, to take his hands and beg him to tell her all that he feared so that she might reassure him of her devotion and her lack of judgment.

"Heaven help me, Miss Brooks, that is *all* I am trying to do," he said, only to close his eyes and jerk his head suddenly. "No, that is not the truth. I am trying to protect you, yes, but in doing so, I am also attempting to shield the worst of myself from you. In that sense, Miss Brooks, I am also attempting to protect myself, which, I confess, must appear to be something of an unfavorable notion."

Ellen silently admitted to herself that such a statement did make her stomach swirl like a raging sea. What was it that he was hiding?

"It seems," Lord Stafford continued with a deep breath, his eyes now closed, "that I have very little choice but to do so. You shall, I am sure, be kind enough to listen, Miss Brooks, but I shall not hold it against you should you decide to walk from this room and be glad—grateful, in fact—that you were spared any deep connection with me."

"I shall listen," Ellen said, barely noticing Lady Newfield as she settled a cup and saucer into her hand. Monotonously, she lifted it to her mouth and took a sip, feeling the warmth of the tea spread through her chest but doing nothing to relieve her deep and anxious worry.

Lord Stafford took in another long breath, looked at her once, and then rose to his feet. It seemed as though he was too ashamed to even look at her, too ashamed to even glance at her as he spoke.

He is to tell me that there is an affection between himself and Lady Moore, Ellen thought to herself as Lord Stafford positioned himself directly in front of the fireplace. *I must be strong. I must maintain my composure, no matter what is said to me, so that I can leave his townhouse in peace.*

"Please, Lord Stafford," she found herself saying, her teacup in her hand. "Pray, begin. Whenever you are ready."

Looking more tormented than Ellen had ever seen him, Lord Stafford gave a curt nod and, with his eyes fixed to a portion of the wall behind her, began to speak.

∾

"AND THUS," Lord Stafford concluded, his voice the

same expressionless tone it had been only a short time before, "I thought it best to end our engagement so that you would not be claimed by this dreadful situation. I could not bear to tell you the truth, nor could I even *consider* marrying you when I was certain that Lady Moore would remain a part of my life—of our lives." He shook his head before raking one hand through his hair, his eyes finally darting towards hers. "In protecting you, I can see that I was also protecting myself, and for that, I should beg your forgiveness. But my only thought, Miss Brooks, was to spare you pain. Yes, there would have been a short time of grief and sorrow at the ending of our betrothal, but thereafter, you would have been free to find someone new who would be a vast improvement on a gentleman such as me."

Ellen took in a few long breaths before she said anything in response. One glance at Lady Newfield told her that there was both a sense of shock and a swell of relief that Ellen herself felt also. She was very glad now to know everything, relieved beyond measure that Lord Stafford did not, in fact, want to marry Lady Moore, but was instead being forced into compliance with her out of fear.

Setting aside her teacup and saucer, Ellen rose to her feet and slowly made her way towards Lord Stafford. His eyes had still not lifted to hers by the time she came within a few steps of him, his head hanging low as if he were waiting for her to throw judgment down hard upon him.

"Stafford," Ellen said as gently as she could. "Why do

you feel such shame over something that you could not have known?"

Slowly, Lord Stafford began to raise his head, his eyes filled with astonishment.

"You believed you were in love with her," Ellen said, finding no pain at such a thought. "Most likely, you were. You gave all you could to her protection, believing that she returned such affections."

"But she resided under my roof, as yet unmarried," Lord Stafford said, a catch in his voice. "I fought a duel— one that I did not need to, as it turns out—and gained this scar to remind me of my foolishness. I gave her my devotion *and* my promise—and my shame is more than I can bear."

Looking up into Lord Stafford's eyes, Ellen felt nothing more than compassion for all he had endured. His shame, she felt, was what bound him to secrecy, to this great fear that, should he speak of it to anyone, he would be turned away from them all. Of course, she knew very well that society *would* be so inclined, making certain that Lord Stafford would never again be a part of the *ton*, given that he had resided with an unmarried young lady for whom he had a strong feeling. Their judgment would, in all probability, force him to do as he had promised and marry Lady Moore just so that she would not remain so disgraced. Ellen had no doubt, given what she had just learned, that Lady Moore would do all she could to manipulate the story to make certain that the *ton* felt great sympathy for her. Forgetting entirely about Lady Newfield's presence and ignoring Lord Repington —who was sitting with a smile so broad that she could hardly fail to notice it—Ellen reached up and gently ran one finger lightly over Lord Stafford's scar.

He stiffened immediately, but Ellen did not flinch. Gently, she felt the puckered skin, the tightness of the mark, and felt her heart fill with sympathy all the more.

"She is the one manipulating you, Lord Stafford," she said, looking deeply into his eyes as her hand fell to his shoulder. "I can see why you thought to spare me such pain, for it is indeed a terrible burden that you bear, but I am not the sort of creature to shrink back from difficulty." Her smile lingered as he closed his eyes, a breath shuddering out from him. "You cannot be expected to deal with this situation alone, Lord Stafford. Will you not allow me to help you? Will you not permit me to do all that I can to be of assistance to you?"

"Why?" His voice was hoarse and rasping. "Why should you show me such kindness?"

"Because I do not see things as you do," Ellen told him honestly. "You see nothing but your shame and your guilt, fearing what is to happen to you and what you are to do regarding Lady Moore. You dread that the knowledge she holds over you will come to light."

"And you do not?"

Ellen smiled. "I will not pretend that there is not some anxiety within me should society come to know of it all, but there is no shame in speaking to me of it." Reaching for his hand, she held it tightly in her own, feeling a flare of joy in her heart that she could not help but express. "In doing so, there is now an understanding between us. There need not be this separation." A sudden doubt stole her joy in a breath. "Unless, that is, you want it still to remain?"

Lord Stafford grasped her other hand in his own. "No, no!" he exclaimed with such fervency that Ellen could not help but laugh with relief. "No, I should not like to remain as we are at present. I am truly, desperately sorry to have had to do so in the first place, but I believed that I was doing the best for you."

"I know," Ellen said softly, her heart thrilled at his words. "I am very glad now that Lady Newfield insisted that I did not give up."

"As am I," Lady Newfield added with such a smile on her face that Ellen laughed again and pulled herself into Lord Stafford's embrace. He held her tightly and she heard him sigh with joy, making her eyes close at the sheer happiness that filled her.

"So," Lady Newfield said practically as Ellen was forced to step back from Lord Stafford's embrace. "What are we to do next?"

No longer quite certain what she should do or what she ought to suggest, Ellen looked up at Lord Stafford, who was, she noticed, wearing an expression of uncertainty, just as she was.

"I think," Lord Repington remarked, looking just as delighted as could be, "that, for the time being, you should not inform anyone of your engagement being renewed." He frowned. "That is, if it *is* so."

There was not a moment of hesitation. "Of course it is," Lord Stafford said, his hand still about Ellen's waist. "But perhaps you are right to suggest that we keep it between ourselves at present."

Ellen nodded. "I shall, of course, inform my mother, but she will not breathe a word to anyone." Her smile slipped. "She is greatly taken up with concern for my father."

Lord Stafford's hand tightened on her waist. "And how does he fare?"

"He is recovering slowly," Ellen replied, smiling up at him. "It is slow and gradual, but I believe, in time, he will recover fully."

He smiled at her. "I am glad to hear it," he said honestly. "You cannot know how terrible my guilt was at leaving you in such a situation. If I could steal the moment back, I would do so without hesitation."

That remark sent a sudden idea straight into Ellen's thoughts. Her eyes widened, and she turned to Lady Newfield, who was watching with interest but saying very little.

"Is that not the solution?" she asked, stepping away from Lord Stafford for a moment. "Is that not the only way that Lord Stafford can be truly freed?"

Lady Newfield frowned, clearly a little confused.

"What is it that you mean, Miss Brooks?" Lord Repington asked as Lord Stafford came a little closer to her. "If you have an idea, please speak it openly."

Knowing that what she was about to suggest was not only unorthodox but could bring a great deal of trouble if they were caught, Ellen took a breath and thought things through. The others waited for her to speak as she searched her mind for any other idea, for any other thought that might reside there—but there was nothing.

"From what I understand, Lord Stafford, Lady

Moore is a proud young lady who takes great pride in ensuring that she is always able to do as she pleases, and arrogant in her control when it comes to manipulating others. At present, she has two items that supposedly prove your agreement and your loyalty to her," she said as Lord Stafford nodded slowly. "The letter you wrote, which contains various details pertaining to your marriage—the marriage that was to be—and the locket."

"I gave her many gifts," Lord Stafford said, his brow furrowed. "But none bore my name or my promise save for those two items."

Ellen nodded, then turned back to Lady Newfield. "Surely, Lady Moore would have them in her possession, would she not? If she has come to persuade Lord Stafford to do as she asks, then she would bring them with her to London."

Lord Repington began to nod slowly. "It would make little sense for her to leave them behind," he said, turning to Lord Stafford. "For what if you demanded proof that she still had such possessions? She could not very well state that she had left them elsewhere."

Turning to face her betrothed, Ellen saw the dark expression that was now etched across his face. Clearly, he was well aware of what she was thinking and was already considering the dangers that would face them should they do so.

"You mean to find those two items and steal them from her," he said as Ellen flushed a little but held her ground.

"I am," she said firmly. "For what else can be done? Without her proof, it is merely the words of a recently widowed woman who believes herself engaged to a gentleman who was once acquainted with her. She might still tell her story to a good many of the *ton*, of course, but not everyone will believe her."

"However, if she had those items to prove it to them, then there would be no doubt," Lady Newfield agreed, surprising Ellen with her almost instant concurrence to what had been expressed so far. "Miss Brooks is quite right. That is the only sure way to remove you from Lady Moore's grip, Lord Stafford."

Lord Stafford considered this for a moment or two, his brows still low over his eyes. He meandered from one side of the fireplace to the other, turning swiftly and continuing on his path every few paces. Ellen held her breath, not sure what he would say and yet believing fully that there was no other way forward for them all.

Eventually, Lord Stafford let out a long sigh and threw up his hands. "It is the only idea that has ever made any sense," he admitted, a little wryly. "It will work, of course, for it will take the power she has from her and render it useless." His eyes caught Ellen's, and he smiled. "You have great intelligence, Miss Brooks, and whilst I am grateful, I must wonder how we are to do such a thing."

Lady Newfield laughed and clapped her hands, shaking away the serious atmosphere in a moment.

"I think you must give Miss Brooks a little more time before you demand such answers from her," she chuckled as Ellen blushed furiously. "She has already given you one excellent idea, and now you demand more?" Seeing how Lord Stafford began to sputter, Lady Newfield laughed again and then beckoned for him to sit down.

"Come, let us order more tea and we shall begin to discuss the matter in earnest," she said, taking hold of the situation. "I am certain that, given a little more thought and a little more tea, we shall be able to conjure the most perfect of solutions!"

CHAPTER ELEVEN

It was torment not to draw near to Miss Brooks, yet despite it, Leonard felt a good deal happier than he had in some days. It did not mean that all was at an end, for he certainly had a good deal more difficulty waiting for him than he could yet imagine. But simply the knowledge that Miss Brooks was now returned to him and that their engagement was resumed brought about such a sense of happiness in amongst his worry that he could hardly contain it. He wanted desperately to speak to someone in the *ton* of it, someone he knew would spread it through the rest of the *beau monde* so that Miss Brooks would no longer deal with any whispers, hurried glances, and the like, but given what he had promised, Leonard had no other choice but to do as he had been asked.

"Good evening, Lord Stafford."

Leonard stiffened but did not otherwise outwardly react. "Lady Moore," he said with a tight smile. "I have not yet received a message from you regarding your debts."

This seemed to make Lady Moore brighten somewhat, for her eyes grew warm and her lips curved at the edges. "They are to be delivered tomorrow," she said, reaching out and touching his arm, giving it a light squeeze. "I am glad that you are so amenable."

Grimacing, Leonard stepped back from her, behaving as he knew she would expect. "It is not as though I have any choice in the matter, Lady Moore."

"No," she purred, clearly enjoying his discomfort. "You do not. Although I must say, it would be much easier for you simply to become engaged to me, as you have promised. We could be wed within the month! And then you would need only to share your wealth, your home, and all your possessions with me as your wife rather than being forced to do so."

Leonard wanted to state that he could not think of anything worse, that he could not even bring himself to imagine what such a life would be, but instead, he remained silent, turning himself away from her.

"Your friend has invited me to his soiree," Lady Moore said offhand. "I am surprised, I confess."

Knowing that this was one of the most important matters regarding their plan, Leonard dropped his brow low and let the anger he felt for Lady Moore reveal itself just a little in his expression. "What are you speaking of?"

This, it seemed, delighted Lady Moore, for her eyes began to sparkle and her lips pulled into an astonished smile. "Do you mean to say that he has not spoken to you of this?"

Leonard's jaw worked furiously. "You mean to say that Lord Repington has included you amongst his invitations?" he bit out, letting his gaze rove across the room in search of his friend. Seeing him, he started forward, but Lady Moore reached out and put one hand on his chest.

"Be wise, Stafford," she said, the smile fading now. "Announce your displeasure at a later time."

"This is more than just displeasure," Leonard retorted, aware that his face was heating but that such a reaction came from her nearness and her willingness to so openly touch him in such a way. His anger was real but not directed towards Lord Repington, even though he was sure it appeared so.

"You dislike that your friend has invited me," Lady Moore crooned, her expression now one of joy at his discomfort, which only made Leonard dislike her all the more. "I do hope he has nothing but the best of intentions in doing so?"

Leonard frowned, stepping back so that she did not need to fear that he would stride across the room towards Lord Repington again. "What do you mean?"

"He will not take an opportunity to express to the *ton* what is between us, I hope," Lady Moore replied lightly. "For if he does, I need not remind you what will happen, do I? You shall find our engagement still stands and that the *beau monde* will wait expectantly for our wedding to take place."

Letting his lip curl, Leonard looked Lady Moore straight in the eye. "Lord Repington understands the need for secrecy in this matter," he said honestly. "He will not do anything such as you have suggested. Most likely, he is attempting to appeal to your good nature—if there is any such thing within you at all."

Lady Moore arched one eyebrow, her eyes glinting, although there was still a small smile on her lips. Miss Brooks had been correct in her thought that any flattery, any suggestion that Lady Moore was perfectly in control, would be tantalizing to her, making her much more likely to feel quite satisfied with all that had been put in place.

"And you are to be there also, it seems?"

Again, Leonard grimaced, his lip curling just a little. "I know what you expect of me, Lady Moore. Knowing that you shall be present, I should like nothing more than to remove myself from the soiree—but I shall be there for a short time, that is all. You cannot expect more."

"Then if there is dancing, I hope we shall be able to dance together," she said, her eyes narrowing just a little. "I shall not stand for your deliberate refusal."

Leonard felt anger burn within him, a tight knot forming in his chest. Lady Moore was deliberately forcing her will upon him, knowing that should he refuse, he would then be standing directly in the path of his own destruction. He made to go past her without answering, but Lady Moore settled one hand on his chest for only a moment, bringing him to a stop.

"We *shall* dance, Lord Stafford."

"Yes," he grated, hating every word that came from his mouth. "Yes, Lady Moore. We shall dance."

Her laugh was light, and yet it seemed to sting him, to reach out and sear his skin as he battled the fury that burned within him.

"Excellent," she cooed, finally allowing him to go past. "Then, I find that I am already looking forward to tomorrow evening with much more anticipation than before."

Making his way across the room and towards Lord Repington, Leonard felt a cold hand grip his heart. Had it not been for Miss Brooks and her suggestion as to how to remove himself from Lady Moore's grip, then this was the life he would now be facing, without any hope of escape. He would be at Lady Moore's beck and call, told what to do and when to do it, knowing that if he did not, she could very easily ruin the rest of his life.

A shudder ran through him. The thought of her being his wife, of him being her husband, was more dire than he could even imagine. How grateful he was now for Miss Brooks, how overwhelmed he was by her loyalty and her understanding. She had shown him more generosity of spirit and kindness of heart than he had ever expected, and he knew now that he would never again let her go. They were as one already, of one spirit, one mind, one thought. Their future was bright, and Leonard could hardly wait to allow it to begin.

"She has spoken to you, then."

"Yes, and I am meant to be furious with you if you recall," Leonard muttered, beginning to gesticulate wildly. "I am certain she is watching."

Lord Repington's eyes darted across the room and then back towards Leonard. "She is, yes," he muttered, putting one hand on Leonard's shoulder, which immediately shrugged off. "Shall we continue to speak in the other room?"

Leonard allowed his hands to fall to his sides, although his fingers still curled into fists as evidence of his anger. "That would suit me very well," he said with relief. "Anything to remove myself from her watchful eye."

Lord Repington looked as though he were about to smile and then quickly rearranged his features so that he would not do so. Turning, he began to make his way through the guests towards the music room, which, Leonard knew, would be a little quieter than the drawing-room. Once there, he allowed himself a long breath of relief and sat down quickly in a vacant chair. Lord Repington grasped two glasses of brandy and handed one to Leonard.

"Lord Wiltshire never skimps on brandy," he said appreciatively. "And it is required all the more at times like this!"

"It is all going as well as we had planned," Leonard muttered, feeling his stomach tighten with nerves. "Although I do wish that it was not Miss Brooks who was to search Lady Moore's home."

Lord Repington smiled sympathetically. "She will have Lady Newfield with her," he reminded Leonard, who nodded slowly. "And this must take place if you are to be free of Lady Moore entirely. You know there is nothing else to be done."

Leonard nodded and took another sip of brandy, keeping one eye on the door for fear that Lady Moore would suddenly make her presence known. "She took great delight in ensuring that I would be present at the soiree and not hiding from her—although," he added, hurriedly, "Lady Moore hopes there will be dancing later in the evening. I am sure that you will oblige."

Lord Repington grinned. "But, of course," he replied with a small inclination of his head. "What else can I do but oblige Lady Moore?"

"Hopefully, it will be for the very last time," Leonard remarked. "Your little soiree cannot come soon enough."

∿

"I—I MUST GO."

Miss Brooks smiled up at him, no sense of tension in her frame, no worry glinting in her eyes.

"You will be quite safe?"

"I will send you the carriage as planned," she said gently, refusing to answer his question. "I am to be with Lady Newfield if you recall? It will all go very well, I am sure of it." Her eyes twinkled. "And thereafter, I must speak to you about my lady's maid, Betty, and one of your staff. I believe there is an affection there that must be permitted to continue!"

Leonard let out a long breath and, holding out his hands to her, waited until she had taken them. Lady Newfield had gone to make certain that Lady Coulbourne had eaten her dinner that evening—or some such excuse—leaving Leonard alone with Miss Brooks, and he knew all too well that the lady was giving him a few moments to speak openly with his betrothed. Miss Brooks was doing her best to distract him from his fears, but, as yet, she was not quite succeeding.

"You need not fear on my account," Miss Brooks said gently, lifting one hand and pressing it to his cheek. "I shall be quite all right, I assure you."

"You cannot be certain of that," he answered, feeling his heart ache within his chest. If only he could take her place! He might then be more at peace, more contented to continue with their plan. "What if she—"

"Lady Moore will be much too busy tormenting you to worry about her staff and her house," Miss Brooks interrupted, letting go of one of his hands and instead pressing it lightly to his cheek. One of her fingers rested on his scar, but Leonard barely noticed it. Miss Brooks accepted him just as he was, and he loved her for that.

"I am sure you are right," Leonard murmured as another sensation swept over him, chasing his anxiety away. There was now a desperate urge to hold Miss Brooks close to him, to make certain that she knew just how important she was to him and how desperately he wanted to make sure that she was safe. "I would do more myself if I could, to spare you the trouble and the difficulty, but I know I cannot."

"Then do stop worrying," Miss Brooks replied with a quick smile, her eyes sparkling. "I am more than capable, I assure you."

His fingers pressed hers as he looked down into her eyes, aware of the quickening of his breath and how his stomach began to tighten with the awareness of her nearness. When she had kissed him before, it had been out of desperation to keep him from ending their engagement. He had known it but had allowed himself that brief joy, even though he had been forced to tear himself away, causing them both a great deal of pain. But now, there was no need for him to fear the consequences of doing so. It would not be a kiss to part with, a kiss to be both a torment and a joy in his memory, but a kiss that would be nothing more than an expression of just how dear Miss Brooks had become to him, of just how much affection he held for her within his own heart.

"You have said nothing for some moments, Lord Stafford," Miss Brooks remarked, a teasing smile curving her lips. "What is it you can be thinking, I wonder?"

Leonard laughed softly, lifting one hand to her cheek, just as she had done. Her skin was warm and soft, a flush coloring her cheeks as his finger ran down the curve of her throat, settling on her shoulder for a moment before he returned to cup her face.

"You are very beautiful, Miss Brooks."

The words came from his mouth without any intention other than to speak what was on his mind.

"I recall you stating that your father always said you were plain, but I can assure you, my dear, that he was and is quite mistaken," he continued softly, as Miss Brooks' blush deepened. "I think you are the most beautiful of ladies, my dear. I am blessed to have found you—and to have gained your hand twice!"

She laughed and moved a little closer, letting go of his other hand and bringing hers to rest gently on his chest. Leonard found his free hand now pulling her closer, his arm about her waist as she looked up into his eyes. His heart was pounding furiously, his anticipation mounting with every passing second, and yet still he lingered, wanting to speak to her of what was on his heart.

"When I first came to you to end our betrothal, you said that you believed I had come to care for you and you for me," he said as she nodded, her hand slipping around his neck, her breath whispering across his cheek. "I admitted to you, I believe, that I had something of that feeling within me, but it was solely because I dared not speak the truth, Miss Brooks."

"Ellen."

His smile was immediate. "Ellen," he said, marveling at the delight it brought him to speak her name aloud. "I dared not speak the truth to you for fear of causing myself and you all the more pain."

Her smile was gentle, her eyes bright with expectation. "But you will speak to me of it now?"

"I will," he answered quietly. "The truth is, Ellen, that I had begun to feel an affection for you that had wound itself through my heart. I knew that I would not be able to remove you from my thoughts and from my heart for the rest of my days, hating what I felt I had to give up instead of being able to hold onto it as I so eagerly desired."

"And now?"

He laughed and pulled her all the closer. "And now I can confess to you the truth," he said honestly. "My dear Ellen, you have more courage, strength, kindness, and wisdom than any other lady of my acquaintance. You have looked at me without judgment, without contempt or fright. I can still recall the day that I met you, fearing that you would look at my scar and would shrink away, would stare at me in horror, just as every other lady had done."

Bending his head low, he brushed a quick kiss across her lips, fighting the urge to linger there. He had more to say, and he wanted desperately to be able to say it all.

"But you did not. You saw it but thought nothing of it. You looked at me as though I were just an ordinary fellow, one without stain or imperfection. I cannot tell you just how much my heart cried out with relief at that moment."

Miss Brooks leaned forward and rested her head on his shoulder, her hand at his neck whilst the other wrapped around him. "I have never seen you as someone imperfect, Stafford," she whispered as he held her. "The relief that came into my heart when you finally told me all, when I knew that there was no reason for us not to continue our engagement, was so vast that I feared I would lose myself within it." She laughed ruefully and lifted her head again. "For some moments, I was dreadfully afraid that you would declare yourself in love with Lady Moore, that you would tell me that she was the only creature you had ever cared for and that her return to London meant you could now pursue her wholeheartedly."

Leonard closed his eyes, grimacing as he did so. He could hardly imagine the pain and the fear that Miss Brooks had endured and felt guilt press hard at his heart.

"Never," he whispered, opening his eyes and lifting both hands to cup Miss Brooks' face. He still had not told her what was in his heart, finding the words creeping up within him, wanting to force themselves from his lips. "I may have believed myself to be in love with Lady Moore, but I know now that it was not so. It was nothing in comparison to what is between us, Ellen. There is an intimacy between us already that was never present with her."

She smiled. "You need not reassure me, Stafford," she whispered softly, her hands now resting on his shoulders. "But if you do not kiss me soon, I think I shall go quite mad!"

His eyes flared with surprise before he began to laugh. This was what he loved about Miss Brooks. She spoke with an openness and a boldness that was absent from so many others of his acquaintance. There was no shyness in her manner, no pretense or manipulation to try and gain what she sought. Instead, she simply spoke of what was in her heart, with a vulnerability that reached out to him. Still, he realized he had not told her all that was within him, had not spoken of all that he wanted to say, but how could he refuse her this when she had asked for it with such expectation in her eyes?

"I shall oblige then, Ellen," he said, laughingly, before pulling her close and settling his lips on hers. She went into his embrace willingly, her arms about his neck, her fingers brushing through his hair. Leonard tilted his head and deepened their kiss, finding himself in danger of being entirely overwhelmed with all that he felt. She was everything to him, and he felt as though he could not breathe without her.

Hearing footsteps, Leonard reluctantly pulled himself back from her, certain that Miss Brooks' flushed cheeks and sparkling eyes would betray what they had been doing.

"There is more I must say to you," he whispered, clutching her hand in his. "But there is time still."

"Once this is at an end," she told him as he lifted her hand to his lips and pressed a kiss to the back of it, "we shall have all the time in the world to speak of what is on our hearts, Stafford."

He smiled, let go of her hand, and made himself take a few steps back from her, giving the appearance of propriety even though he was certain Lady Newfield would be able to guess what had occurred. "Then let that time come all the quicker, Miss Brooks," he said just as Lady Newfield walked into the room. "For I am not certain I can wait much longer."

CHAPTER TWELVE

"You are smiling to yourself again."

Ellen laughed and pressed one hand to her flushed cheeks. "Indeed, it seems that I am."

"Lord Stafford must have been very...comforting in all he had to say," Lady Newfield remarked, a knowing smile playing about her mouth as they sat in the carriage, the dim light of the lanterns illuminating her features briefly. "I am glad you had the opportunity to talk, however."

Ellen nodded but said nothing more. There *had* been an opportunity for them both to speak at length, but there was, as Lord Stafford had said, more for them to say. She was quite certain that she knew what he would say to her, for she had the very same desire within her own heart. There was a love for him that had grown furiously over the last few days, a love that seemed to burn up through her whenever she saw him. And yet, there had not been the time to express it. She had felt herself eager for his kiss, had waited for him to press his lips to hers once more, and when he had finally done so, it had been as though everything about them had burst into life at once. She had been aware of him in a way that she had never truly experienced before. Their first kiss had been one born of sheer desperation, whereas this one had been a coming together of two hearts, bringing with it happiness that tied them together.

"And now we must think of what we are to do this evening," Lady Newfield said, bringing Ellen's attention back to their task at hand. "We cannot lose our intention from our minds for even a single moment."

Nodding, Ellen tried to push Lord Stafford from her mind, feeling a sudden wave of anxiety flood her as the carriage began to slow. "I understand, Lady Newfield."

"If you wish it, I shall take your place," Lady Newfield said, looking keenly at Ellen. "You need only sit in the chair and make excuses as to my whereabouts, should anyone ask."

Ellen took in a deep breath and settled her anxiety. She pushed it aside and focused solely on Lord Stafford. This was something that she had to do, to make certain that the gentleman she had come to care for with such a deep and unrelenting passion was freed from a situation that was not of his own making.

"I shall be quite all right," she told Lady Newfield, her voice steadier than she had expected. "I think any of Lady Moore's staff will be more than willing to listen to you, given that you have such authority, whereas I might fumble and search about for any excuse as to why you are absent."

Lady Newfield smiled, reached across and patted

Ellen's hand reassuringly. "You will do very well, and achieve precisely what we have come to do," she said without any hint of doubt in either her words or her expression. "Come now. We have arrived."

Having instructed a small beggar child to come to inform her the moment Lady Moore left the house—and having paid him handsomely for his trouble—Ellen stepped out of the carriage with a certainty that Lady Moore would not be at home. Had they simply appeared at the door without assurance that she was not present, then all might have gone spectacularly wrong before they had even had the opportunity to begin! Taking in a deep breath, Ellen lifted her chin and climbed the stone steps, lifting her skirts carefully. Lady Newfield came after her and, together, they stood at the door.

"Recall your expression, Miss Brooks," Lady Newfield reminded her, and quickly, Ellen dropped her head, forcing a sadness to her face that was not truly felt. "Very good," she heard Lady Newfield say, a note of mirth in her voice. "Now. Let us begin."

She rapped sharply on the door, and Ellen's heart leaped with a sudden fright. Would the door be opened to them? It might be that the staff had retired for the evening, although usually, one or two remained on duty to prepare for their master or mistress' return.

They were in luck, it seemed, for the door opened shortly after they had knocked, revealing a man Ellen took to be the butler.

"Ah, wonderful," Lady Newfield said with a note of exasperation. "Where is your mistress? I must speak to her at once."

The butler said nothing for a moment, his eyes rounding a little as he took in Ellen's distressed face and Lady Newfield's hard gaze.

"Lady Moore has gone out for the evening," he said, opening the door a little wider so that he might speak to them better. "I am sorry, but she will not return until a good deal later."

Lady Newfield drew herself up to her full height. "It is *imperative* that I speak to her," she said sharply. "Do you not understand? Am I making myself somehow unclear?"

The butler shook his head, opening his mouth to state, no doubt, that there was nothing he could do, but before he could say a single word, Lady Newfield stepped forward. Pushing the door open wide, she stepped inside without hesitation, leaving Ellen to follow —whilst the poor butler could only stammer helplessly.

"I am *terribly* sorry," the butler said as Lady Newfield looked at him expectantly, "but Lady Moore may not return until the early hours of the morning." He spread his hands, evidently praying that this would be enough to remove both Ellen and Lady Newfield from his mistress' house. "I can, of course, inform her that you were present and needed to speak to her most urgently."

"We will wait," Lady Newfield said firmly, removing her gloves and handing them to the startled butler. "You need not worry about our comfort. Show us to the library, perhaps, so that we might read until your mistress returns. And have some tea and refreshments sent also." Gesturing to Ellen, she let out a heavy sigh. "As I have said, it is of the greatest importance that we speak to your mistress this evening."

The butler blinked rapidly, clearly not at all certain what it was he was meant to say in response to this—but Ellen merely handed him her particulars also, and gave a small, sad sniff as she did so.

"Should I send for Lady Moore?" the butler asked after a long moment, clearly no longer able to find any way to suggest that they depart. "If it is of such importance, then mayhap she will—"

"Certainly not," Lady Newfield snapped, rounding on him as though he had suggested something most improper. "Your mistress must be allowed to enjoy her evening. As I have stated, with refreshments and something to read, we will be more than contented to wait until she returns, no matter what the hour."

And so, within the next quarter of an hour, Ellen found herself seated in Lady Moore's library with a tray of hastily prepared cakes and other delicacies in front of her. Another maid was busy setting out the tea things, all whilst Lady Newfield watched on with a sharp eye. Ellen kept her head low, recalling that she was still meant to be deeply upset. She had to admire Lady Newfield, for without her firm direction and her stern manner, Ellen did not think that they would be seated where they were. Lady Newfield had pushed her way into the house and then refused to be moved from it! There was a great deal of strength in the older lady, and Ellen could not help but respect such a characteristic. In fact, she contemplated, as Lady Newfield dismissed the maid, without Lady Newfield, there might not have been any reconciliation between herself and Lord Stafford. She might now find herself lost and broken with the sorrow and the pain of his crying off rather than filled with hope and happy expectation for the future.

"At last, we are alone!" Lady Newfield exclaimed as the door closed behind the maid. "Now, the staff, I think, will have retired—most of them, anyway. The butler and the lady's maid will still be around, waiting for Lady Moore's return."

"The lady's maid might be in Lady Moore's bedchamber, then," Ellen answered, rising from her chair and making her way slowly towards the door. "What shall I do if she is present?"

Lady Newfield smiled and shrugged one shoulder. "Whatever you must!" she replied with a laugh. "I shall search here in the library, but my expectation is that you shall find both document and locket within Lady Moore's bedchamber."

Now that the task was at hand, it seemed almost entirely insurmountable. What was she thinking? Could she really search an entire bedchamber on her own, seeking two things that would, most likely, be hidden away? Nerves clawed at her belly, her whole body trembling violently for a moment as she placed one hand on the door handle. Taking in a deep breath and glancing back at Lady Newfield, who gave her an encouraging smile, Ellen turned the handle carefully and opened the door.

The hallway was quiet. There appeared to be no staff present, for there were no footmen at the door, nor maids making their way to and fro.

I am seeking the retiring room; I am seeking the retiring room, Ellen reminded herself as she slowly closed the door behind her. That was what she had planned to say to anyone who found her wandering through Lady Moore's house, for it was a decent excuse and certainly one that would have no one asking her any particular questions. All they would do would be to show her to the room and then leave her in peace.

Looking all about her, Ellen padded forward on quiet feet. Most likely, Lady Moore's bedchamber would be upstairs, meaning that she would have to climb the stair-case. Thankfully, the house was not overly large—the library was small, and she expected the rest of the rooms to be so also. However, climbing the staircase meant that she would have nowhere to hide should one of the servants find her, and her excuse of seeking the retiring room might not be as acceptable, given that she had no need to be climbing the staircase to the upstairs in search of it.

This was your plan, Ellen, she told herself, harnessing her courage. *Now do hurry up!*

With a grim smile, and knowing that every moment was precious, Ellen hurried forward and, without a back-ward glance, began to climb the stairs. Her skirts rustled in a most infuriating manner, but Ellen did not pause for a moment. Hurrying to the very top, she took a moment to look all about her, aware of the hurried thud of her heart.

I must be bold.

The door immediately to her left would not, Ellen thought, be Lady Moore's bedchamber, for it was much too close to the staircase. She would be in danger of hearing the comings and goings of the staff early in the morning. Thus, Ellen continued to make her way slowly along the hallway, aware that, very soon, she was to come to the end. There was another door to her left and one in front, but that was all. She could not guess which one might be Lady Moore's bedchamber. Stepping to her left, she turned the door handle carefully, hearing the door creak as it opened and wincing furiously as she stepped inside.

The room was in complete darkness. Ellen frowned, pushing the door open a little more but finding not even the smallest bit of light anywhere. Surely this could not be Lady Moore's bedchamber? It was much too cold, and she would expect there to be at least one candle lit, ready and waiting for her.

Unless she is being economical, Ellen thought to herself, remembering what Lord Stafford had said about Lady Moore being left with very little by her late husband. Perhaps she did not want a candle lit in preparation. Mayhap she was doing what she could to save.

The sound of someone climbing the stairs made Ellen's heart slam into her chest furiously. Panicked, she turned back and pushed the door closed, although not tightly. Closing her eyes and praying that the person coming towards her would not notice the door, Ellen pressed herself against the wall and squeezed her eyes shut.

The steps grew a little louder, as well as, she realized, the sound of someone's voice. Were there two people present?

"I should like to know what she thinks she's doing, making us..."

The voice trailed away as the footsteps went past Ellen's door. No, there were not two people present. Rather, there was only one, and they, it seemed, were complaining furiously about someone—most likely, Lady Moore.

Letting out a long breath, Ellen kept her eyes closed but listened hard. She could hear nothing for some time but did not dare come out, realizing that the maid must have gone into the other room. That did not bode well for her, for she could not hide for the rest of the evening! No doubt, the butler would soon come to check that both she and Lady Newfield were quite settled, and Lady Newfield could not make the same excuse twice.

She did not know how long she stood there. Her hands pressed against the cold wall, making her shiver, but still, she did not move. Waiting patiently, there came such a rush of relief when she heard the door opening again and the same muttering voice making its way past her that Ellen felt the need to sit down to rest herself for a few moments.

But she dared not. If the maid had gone to prepare Lady Moore's room, then there would be no reason for her to return until her mistress had come home. Letting out a slow breath, Ellen carefully pulled the door open again and stepped out into the hallway.

There was no one in sight.

With quick steps, Ellen hurried towards the other door, hesitating for only a moment before turning the door handle and pushing it open.

I must be bold.

Her mind scrambled for some excuse to give should the maid be within, but much to her relief, there was no one present at all. The room was lit with candles, with a small fire burning in the grate, already bringing a warmth to the chill that was so often felt in the night air. Satisfied that she had discovered the room she was in search of, Ellen pushed the door closed and settled back upon it for a moment as she took in the place.

There was everything one might expect within a bedchamber. The dressing table stood ready for her mistress' return, the bed already fully prepared for Lady Moore to climb into. Ellen also took in the wardrobe, which, no doubt, would be full of gowns for Lady Moore to choose from.

"That would be a place to hide," she muttered to herself, stepping away from the door and moving a little further forward into the room. Looking all about her, she sat down first at the dressing table, glancing at herself in the mirror.

Her cheeks were flushed, her eyes bright but her lips pulled into a tight line that betrayed her anxiety. With a deep breath, Ellen turned to the drawers and pulled them out one at a time. She did not want to have to dig through Lady Moore's things, but at a time like this, there was no need for propriety.

Picking up what appeared to be a few letters tied with a ribbon, Ellen picked them up and set them on the dressing table—only for her eye to catch something.

"It cannot be!" she breathed, seeing the flash of gold underneath what appeared to be a folded letter tied with a ribbon. Her heart began to beat furiously as she picked up the letter and saw, much to her astonishment, a gold locket.

"She cannot have been this foolish!" Ellen exclaimed, picking up the locket and turning it over in her hand. It was, she realized, the very locket that Lord Stafford had given to Lady Moore. The inscription was just as he had explained, making her heart twist as she read it. It was not because she felt any jealousy towards him but rather that there was a sense of sadness in what she read. Sadness that Lord Stafford had trusted Lady Moore so implicitly and had been led to believe that she cared for him also, only to find his entire life shattered by her lies.

Placing the locket carefully on the dressing table, Ellen looked back in the drawer but saw that it was empty. Her heart began to flutter in panic, worrying that she would only be able to find one out of the two items— only to realize that the ribbon-tied letter she had lifted out from it in order to see the locket was, in fact, the one that held the promises from Lord Stafford. Lady Moore had clearly never expected anyone to come searching through her things, and thus had kept these two items together where she might easily access them. Picking up both items, she pressed them into her pocket and made to set the other stack of letters back into the drawer, only for a stab of curiosity to catch her.

Setting them back down again, she untied the ribbon that held them all together and picked up one. With a glance behind her, as though someone would be watching her do something as improper as reading another lady's letters, she unfolded it and skimmed the contents.

Her heart quickened. Without needing to read any further, she hurriedly folded it back up and placed it with the others. With trembling fingers, she tied the ribbon again and picked them up. Placing them in her other gown pocket, Ellen lifted her chin and drew in a long breath. Now all she had to do was return to Lady Newfield.

~

"Ah, she has returned."

Ellen stepped back into the library with what she hoped was an innocent look. The butler turned to face her, bowing his head as he did so.

"You are comfortable now, I hope?" Lady Newfield asked as Ellen dropped her head and murmured something that sounded like an agreement. "Good. The butler had come to ensure that we had everything we required."

Seeing that her tea was now sitting waiting for her—no doubt, cold by now—Ellen sat down quickly and picked it up, taking a small sip.

"Some more tea, perhaps?" Lady Newfield suggested as the butler nodded his head. "That would be most welcome."

"But of course," he replied, looking relieved that Ellen had returned. "Excuse me."

Lady Newfield said nothing but waved her hand in dismissal. Ellen smiled at her friend as the butler closed the door behind her, although a flicker of anxiety still remained.

"Had he been waiting here long?" she asked as Lady

Newfield shook her head. "I was as quick as I could be. I also went to the door and signaled to the driver. He has already departed."

Lady Newfield picked up her teacup and took a sip, setting it down again and giving herself a slight shake as though to settle her own nerves.

"The butler was in here for only a few moments before you arrived," she said, much to Ellen's relief. "I stated that you had gone to the retiring room, and that seemed to satisfy him. Although if you had been much longer, I am not certain what would have occurred!" She smiled at Ellen, her voice now a little more excited. "I can tell from your expression and from what you have said that you have done well, I think!"

Ellen nodded. "I could hardly believe my luck," she said, quickly explaining what occurred. "To leave them in such an obvious place rather than hide them away!"

Lady Newfield shrugged, her eyes a little dark. "The lady is clearly arrogant enough to believe that she will succeed no matter what," she said. "To keep such precious items nearby means that she does not believe she is in any danger of failing. All is well, as far as Lady Moore is concerned." She sat back in her chair with a sigh of contentment leaving her lips. "But she shall soon learn that it is not so."

Taking another sip of her lukewarm tea and realizing just how parched she was, Ellen pulled out the letters from her gown pocket and handed them to Lady Newfield.

"I took these also," she said by way of explanation. "They were kept with the locket and the note."

Lady Newfield frowned. "What are they?"

Ellen shook her head, darkness gripping her heart for a moment. "Lady Moore has received letters of adoration —and most likely, letters of promise, similar to Lord Stafford's—from other gentlemen of the *ton*. I would presume that, should things ever become difficult for her, she would use them in the same manner."

Taking one out and reading it quickly, Lady Newfield's eyes widened, and she turned to look at Ellen. "Goodness," she murmured, refolding the letter and setting it back in with the others. "Then it seems that you have saved not only Lord Stafford, Miss Brooks, but other gentlemen along with him who now, unwittingly, owe you a great debt."

"Let us hope that the rest of the evening goes just as well," Ellen remarked, just as the door opened to reveal the butler with a tea tray for them both. "I shall be very glad indeed if we have success."

"I am certain we shall," Lady Newfield remarked as the butler set down the tray. "The difficult part is over. Now, all we need do is wait."

CHAPTER THIRTEEN

T he evening had gone very well, indeed. Lady
Moore had been present for many hours now and
showed no sign of leaving the soiree. Lord Repington had
been an excellent host, and now that it was time for the
guests to return home, Leonard found himself growing a
trifle anxious. Would the carriage be waiting there? That
was to be the signal that said Lady Newfield and Miss
Brooks had been successful. If Lady Newfield's carriage
was waiting for him, then he had to ensure he made his
way to Lady Moore's home. If there was no carriage, then
she had not found what she had been seeking.

"And we are the last to depart," Lady Moore said, her
eyes fixing to his, although her smile sent a chill through
him. "Are you to remain with Lord Repington for a
time?"

Leonard looked away from her. "If I choose," he
stated as Lady Moore leaned against him in an overt
manner, making him step away from her. "Good evening,
Lady Moore."

She laughed, and Leonard felt a jolt run through him. That laugh would no longer torment him, had Miss Brooks succeeded. He had spent the evening doing everything Lady Moore wished, dancing with her, conversing with her when she asked, albeit with a great deal of darkness in his expression and a less than pleasing manner when he spoke. It had been his duty, as far as Lady Moore was concerned, for she could not possibly know that he had been eager to keep her in his sight at all times, to make certain that she did not slip away without his knowledge.

"And you have begun to pay my debts already, I hear," Lady Moore murmured, looking at him with a curling smile that made him want to turn away from her entirely. "How very good of you, Lord Stafford."

He said nothing. He had received her list of debts and had, for appearance's sake only, paid for the smallest debt he could find. Lady Moore's debts were significant, and he knew full well that, if he did not pay them for her, then she would be left with very little indeed. Even the townhouse she resided in at present was not her own, for the new Lord Moore had allowed her to stay for the Season, but no longer. What she was to do thereafter, Leonard did not want to imagine. No doubt, he was in her plans—although he prayed that it would not be so for long.

"Good evening, Lady Moore," he said again as Lord Repington turned to her, ready to make his final farewell as he had done with all the other guests.

Leonard watched her depart, all too aware of the glance over her shoulder towards him before she took her leave. The moment she had climbed into her carriage, he was there beside Lord Repington, looking out into the darkness.

"It is there," Lord Repington said with a broad smile. "The carriage is waiting for us."

Letting out a huge breath of relief, Leonard grinned at his friend and then hurried down the steps, Lord Repington at his heels. His freedom was within his reach. Miss Brooks had found what she had been searching for. The nightmare would soon be at an end.

"Do allow us in."

Without waiting for the butler to say anything, Leonard pushed his way into the house, Lord Repington just behind him.

"Where is Lady Moore?" he asked as the butler stared wide-eyed at him. "She is speaking to Lady Newfield and Miss Brooks, is she not?"

The man blinked rapidly, clearly overcome with confusion at this strange arrival, so late at night.

"In—in the library, my lord," he said faintly, gesturing down the hallway. "Might I fetch you a brandy?"

Leonard did not answer him, striding down the hallway until he heard the sound of voices coming from one of the rooms. Turning the handle, he pushed the door open wide and stepped inside.

"Lord Stafford!" Lady Moore exclaimed, turning towards him with a quickly produced smile that Leonard knew covered the truth of what she was feeling. "You have chased after me, it seems!" She laughed softly and came towards him, gesturing to where Lady Newfield and Miss Brooks sat. "But you have come at an already busy time, it seems! I have guests—although, as yet, I am uncertain as to why."

Hearing Lord Repington shut the door behind them all, Leonard ignored Lady Moore, walking past her and coming directly to Miss Brooks, who at once rose to greet him.

"You have succeeded, then?" he asked, pulling her into his arms and holding her close for a long moment. Leaning back, he looked into her eyes and saw her smile. His heart tore from his chest with exultation, and he could not help but kiss her soundly, making Miss Brooks laugh as he finally released her.

Turning back to face Lady Moore, Leonard was satisfied to see the stunned expression and the paleness of her cheeks.

"Might I introduce my betrothed, Lady Moore?" he said as she stared at him in confusion. "I am sure that you heard that I cried off." He waved a hand. "That has been clarified, however, although not many know of it." Squeezing Miss Brooks' hand, he looked back to smile at her. "I love Miss Brooks desperately, and she is to be my bride."

For a moment, nothing was said. Lady Moore's gaze traveled from his features to Miss Brooks' face and then back again. There was no smile on her face now, nothing in her features that spoke of delight. Instead, there was complete and utter shock—and Leonard had never felt such a sense of triumph.

"Then I hope," Lady Moore said, recovering herself a little, "that Miss Brooks is fully aware of all that you owe to me?" She arched one eyebrow delicately but then made to sit down, smoothing her skirts as she did so. "You must be aware, Miss Brooks, that Lord Stafford has promised himself to me."

Leonard made to say something, only to hear Miss Brooks laugh. She stepped forward, closer to him, and he slipped one hand about her waist as she spoke. They were standing together now, strong and determined, and he knew for certain that all Lady Moore thought she had would soon come tumbling down around her in a heap.

"I have heard the truth about you, Lady Moore," Miss Brooks began quietly. "I have heard it all. Lord Stafford has not hidden it from me." She gestured to Lord Repington and then to Lady Newfield. "Indeed, we are *all* aware of it. And, given that my heart is entirely given to Lord Stafford, I could not rest until we discovered a way to remove you from him."

Lady Moore shook her head and sighed in an almost compassionate sense, as though she pitied Miss Brooks. "But what can you do?" she asked, with a flutter of her fingers. "I have the proof of his intentions towards me, and there is nothing that—"

"Yes, the promise he wrote and the locket that he inscribed," Miss Brooks interrupted, pulling both from her pocket and, with a smile, handing them to Leonard. "But what shall happen, Lady Moore, when you do not have either of those in your possession any longer?"

Lady Moore's face froze in an expression of horror. Her eyes were wide and fixed on the locket that Leonard let dangle from his fingers. Her mouth was slack, her pallor a little gray as she tried to take in what she saw.

"You shall have only your word, Lady Moore," Leonard said, keeping his voice quiet yet feeling the force of every syllable as they left him. "And that, I am afraid, means very little."

Lady Moore began to shake her head, but from where he stood, Leonard could see that she was shaking.

"How dare you?" she whispered as Leonard shrugged. "How dare you come and *steal* from me!"

"I hardly think you are able to call down judgment upon us since you have been blackmailing Lord Stafford —and having done a good deal more prior to that," Lady Newfield said calmly, tilting her head as though studying Lady Moore's reaction. "Can you really have any sort of remark or condemnation for our actions when you have behaved so despicably?"

Leonard clasped the locket tightly in his hand. It brought so many painful memories with it. Memories of how he had planned it, how he had paid for the many hours of labor that had gone into making such a piece. And how happy he had been when he had given it to her, how much supposed joy had been in her eyes.

He knew now that it had been nothing but a lie. The lady before him had never truly held his heart, for he had not known her. The precious gift he had given her had turned into something cruel and evil. He could not wait to throw it into the depths of the Thames.

"This paper," he said, letting go of Miss Brooks' hand and holding it up for Lady Moore to see, "is filled with words of love and devotion. It promises you that we shall be joined as man and wife, no matter the circumstances, no matter how difficult things may be." Making his way towards the fireplace where candles burned on the mantlepiece, he held the paper out towards the flame and looked directly at Lady Moore. She started from her chair as though intending to pull it from him, only to realize that she could do nothing to save it.

"You broke your word to me," he said as the flame began to lick the edges of the paper. "You lied. You used all your wiles to manipulate me into believing that I cared for you simply so you could gain what you wished—but when another gentleman came along, one who had greater wealth than I, you held onto my promises in the hope that, one day, you would be able to use them against me."

With satisfaction growing in his heart, he watched the flame consume the paper, feeling the heat against his fingers. "It is over now, Lady Moore. There is nothing between us any longer. Nothing you can hold against me, nothing you can do to force my hand." Dropping the rest of the paper onto the mantlepiece, he let it burn until it was nothing but ash, seeing the smoke beginning to rise up from it. "It is at an end, Lady Moore." His smile was one of sheer relief, and he held his hand out to Miss Brooks, who came towards him at once. "Those debts will be returned to you. I shall not do as you ask any longer. I intend, now, to live my life with this magnificent young lady who, I know, shall never betray me."

Miss Brooks smiled at him as he kissed her hand. "Never," she said, her voice clear. "I came to seek you once. You know that I would do so again."

"I do," he assured her, kissing her gently. "Come now. Our matters here are at an end." He smiled at Lady Newfield, who let out a satisfied sigh as she rose from her chair, beaming at Lord Repington as he offered her his arm. "Good evening, Lady Moore. I do hope to never be in your company again."

They made their way to the door, only to be halted by Lady Moore's rasping voice.

"You have done nothing," she said hoarsely, turning to face him. "You may have removed yourself from my grasp, but do not for a moment think that there are not others I can use." She rose a little unsteadily from her chair, turning to them all. With a lift of her chin, she regarded them all as though she were a queen ruling her dominion, and they were nothing more than her servants. "You cannot think, Stafford, that you are the *only* gentleman within my view."

Leonard's stomach dropped. He had not thought for a moment that Lady Moore would have done the same to others, had not once imagined that she could have done so.

"And so you see," Lady Moore continued with a supercilious smile. "Again, Lord Stafford, I shall be the victor."

Not knowing what to say, Leonard stared blankly at Lady Moore, feeling as though some of their triumph had been snatched away. Lady Moore, it seemed, had more at play than he had expected.

"Lady Moore," Miss Brooks said, stepping forward, "I sincerely hope you are not referring to the letters of love and affection that you have collected from, I am sure, *various* gentlemen of the *beau monde*?"

Lady Moore's smile began to slip away as Lady Newfield came to stand beside Miss Brooks, pulling a stack of letters tied with a ribbon from her pocket.

"You did not think that I would leave such letters behind, did you?" Miss Brooks said, no trace of a smile on her face. "Those poor gentlemen would be treated just as Lord Stafford has, and I could not permit it."

Lady Moore drew in a sharp breath, her hand reaching out to lean on a chair for support. "But—but I shall have nothing."

Leonard came to stand next to Miss Brooks, looking directly at Lady Moore. "I think you will find, Lady Moore, that you never had anything in the first place."

"Good afternoon, Lord Stafford."

Leonard hurried towards Miss Brooks at once, his hands outstretched towards her. There had been so little time for them to talk last evening. Given the late hour, Lady Newfield had been required to return Miss Brooks to her townhouse almost at once.

"Ellen," he breathed, lifting both hands to his lips and kissing them one after the other. "Are you well?"

Her smile was dazzling. "Very well indeed," she told him, glancing over her shoulder. "Lady Newfield has thought to give us a few minutes to talk before she attends also. I know she is also very relieved that all has turned out as well as it did."

"As am I," he told her, grateful beyond measure for all she had done. "And your mother is pleased with our engagement?"

"I do not think she could be more delighted," came the reply. "What makes things all the better is that my father is much improved. His speech is getting better every day, and he is able to sit up without difficulty." She sighed contentedly. "I am happier now than I think I have ever been."

"As am I," he told her, honestly. "Without your wisdom, your kindness, your courage, and your determination, I would not have achieved this state of contentment. To know that there is nothing more that can trouble me regarding Lady Moore has given me such a sense of freedom that it is as though I have begun life anew—and it is all because of you."

Miss Brooks smiled up at him. "I think we have achieved this together, Stafford," she said contentedly. "I will confess to feeling anxious when it came to searching Lady Moore's townhouse, but it appears that her foolishness and overconfidence made things so much easier than I had expected. You were the one to suggest Lord Repington throw a soiree so that you might make certain she would depart from her townhouse. And you thought of the carriage to signal our success and spoke to Lady Moore at the end of it all."

"But still," he answered, not allowing her to shun any of the recognition than she deserved, "such a plan would never have come to pass without you at the very first, Ellen. I do not know what I have done to deserve you, but

I am determined that, no matter what else might befall us, I shall love you every day of my life."

He saw the moment that she understood what he had said. Her eyes widened just a fraction, her hand reached out, her fingers touching his with infinite gentleness, as though she could hardly believe what he had said.

"In case you are not certain what I said, Ellen," he murmured, grasping her hands and pulling her close to him. "I love you. Most passionately. My heart shall never be the same again. From the very first moment I met you, I felt something change within me—and that change has brought only goodness, happiness, and contentment with it. You have changed my life completely, Ellen, and I can hardly wait until we take our vows and become husband and wife."

He had barely finished speaking before she wrapped her arms around his neck and stood on tiptoe, her lips to his. She lingered there for some moments, and Leonard kissed her ardently, his heart quickening with the sheer joy of being close to her.

"You know that I love you too," she murmured, pulling back just a little. "When we first met, I was so very afraid that it would not be a good match, but now I am so very glad that my father made such a choice. I did not imagine that I should ever find such joy."

"I feel the very same," he told her, his arms still about her. "And our happiness will continue every day of our lives together. Of that, I have no doubt."

MY DEAR READER

Thank you for reading and supporting my books! I hope this story brought you some escape from the real world into the always captivating Regency world. A good story, especially one with a happy ending, just brightens your day and makes you feel good! If you enjoyed the book, would you leave a review on Amazon? Reviews are always appreciated.

Below is a complete list of all my books! Why not click and see if one of them can keep you entertained for a few hours?

The Rogue's Flower
Saved by the Scoundrel
Mending the Duke
The Baron's Malady

The Returned Lords of Grosvenor Square
The Returned Lords of Grosvenor Square: A Regency
Romance Boxset
The Waiting Bride
The Long Return
The Duke's Saving Grace
A New Home for the Duke

The Spinsters Guild
A New Beginning
The Disgraced Bride
A Gentleman's Revenge
A Foolish Wager
A Lord Undone

Convenient Arrangements
A Broken Betrothal
In Search of Love
Wed in Disgrace
Betrayal and Lies
A Past to Forget

Christmas Stories
Love and Christmas Wishes: Three Regency Romance
Novellas
A Family for Christmas

Mistletoe Magic: A Regency Romance
Home for Christmas Series Page

Happy Reading!

All my love,

Rose

A SNEAK PEAK OF A BROKEN BETROTHAL

PROLOGUE

Lady Augusta looked at her reflection in the mirror and sighed inwardly. She had tried on almost every gown in her wardrobe and still was not at all decided on which one she ought to wear tonight. She had to make the right decision, given that this evening was to be her first outing into society since she had returned to London.

"Augusta, what in heaven's name...?" The sound of her mother's voice fading away as she looked all about the room and saw various gowns strewn everywhere, the maids quickening to stand straight, their heads bowed as the countess came into the room. Along with her came a friend of Lady Elmsworth, whom Augusta knew very well indeed, although it was rather embarrassing to have her step into the bedchamber when it was in such a disarray!

"Good afternoon, Mama," Augusta said, dropping into a quick curtsy. "And good afternoon, Lady Newfield." She took in Lady Newfield's face, seeing the twinkle in the lady's blue eyes and the way her lips twitched, which was in direct contrast to her mother, who was standing with her hands on her hips, clearly upset.

"Would you like to explain, my dear girl, what it is that you are doing here?" The countess looked into Augusta's face, her familiar dark eyes sharpening. Augusta tried to smile but her mother only narrowed her eyes and planted her hands on her hips, making it quite plain that she was greatly displeased with what Augusta was doing.

"Mama," Augusta wheedled, gesturing to her gowns. "You know that I must look my very best for this evening's ball. "Therefore, I must be certain that I—"

"We had already selected a gown, Augusta," Lady Elmsworth interrupted, quieting Augusta's excuses immediately. "You and I went to the dressmaker's only last week and purchased a few gowns that would be worn for this little Season. The first gown you were to wear was, if I recall, that primrose yellow." She indicated a gown that was draped over Augusta's bed, and Augusta felt heat rise into her face as the maids scurried to pick it up.

"I do not think it suits my coloring, Mama," she said, a little half-heartedly. "You are correct to state that we chose it together, but I have since reconsidered."

Lady Newfield cleared her throat, with Lady Elmsworth darting a quick look towards her.

"I would be inclined to agree, Lady Elmsworth," she said, only for Lady Elmsworth to throw up one hand, bringing her friend's words to a swift end. Augusta's hopes died away as her mother's thin brows began knitting together with displeasure. "That is enough, Augusta," she said firmly, ignoring Lady Newfield entirely. "That gown will do you very well, just as we discussed." She looked at the maids. "Tidy the rest of these up at once and ensure that the primrose yellow is left for this evening."

The maids curtsied and immediately set to their task, leaving Augusta to merely sit and watch as the maids obeyed the mistress of the house rather than doing what she wanted. In truth, the gown that had been chosen for her had been mostly her mother's choice, whilst she had attempted to make gentle protests that had mostly been ignored. With her dark brown hair and green eyes, Augusta was sure that the gown did, in fact, suit her coloring very well, but she did not want to be clad in yellow, not when so many other debutantes would be wearing the same. No, Augusta wanted to stand out, to be set apart, to be noticed! She had come to London only a few months ago for the Season and had been delighted when her father had encouraged them to return for the little Season. Thus, she had every expectation of finding a suitable husband and making a good match. However, given how particular her mother was being over her gown, Augusta began to worry that her mother would soon begin to choose Augusta's dance partners and the like so that she would have no independence whatsoever!

"I think I shall return to our tea," Lady Newfield said gently as Lady Elmsworth gave her friend a jerky nod. "I apologize for the intrusion, Lady Augusta."

"There was no intrusion," Augusta said quickly, seeing the small smile that ran around Lady Newfield's mouth and wishing that her mother had been a little more willing to listen to her friend's comments. For whatever reason, she felt as though Lady Newfield understood her reasoning more than her mother did.

"Now, Augusta," Lady Elmsworth said firmly, settling herself in a chair near to the hearth where a fire burned brightly, chasing away the chill of a damp winter afternoon. "This evening, you are to be introduced to one gentleman in particular. I want you to ensure that you behave impeccably. Greet him warmly and correctly, but thereafter, do not say a good deal."

Augusta frowned, her eyes searching her mother's face for answers that Lady Elmsworth was clearly unwilling to give. "Might I ask why I am to do such a thing, Mama?"

Lady Elmsworth held Augusta's gaze for a moment, and then let out a small sigh. "You will be displeased, of course, for you are always an ungrateful sort but nonetheless, you ought to find some contentment in this." She waited a moment as though waiting to see if Augusta had some retort prepared already, only to shrug and then continue. "Your father has found you a suitable match, Augusta. You are to meet him this evening."

The world seemed to stop completely as Augusta stared at her mother in horror. The footsteps of the maids came to silence; the quiet crackling of the fire turned to naught. Her chest heaved with great breaths as Augusta tried to accept what she had just been told, closing her eyes to shut out the view of her mother's slightly bored expression. This was not what she had expected. Coming back to London had been a matter of great excitement for her, having been told that *this* year would be the year for her to make a suitable match. She had never once thought that such a thing would be pulled from her, removed from her grasp entirely. Her father had never once mentioned that he would be doing such a thing but now, it seemed, he had chosen to do so without saying a word to her about his intentions.

"Do try to form some response, Augusta," Lady Elmsworth said tiredly. "I am aware this is something of a surprise, but it is for your own good. The gentleman in question has an excellent title and is quite wealthy." She waved a hand in front of her face as though such things were the only things in the world that mattered. "It is not as though you could have found someone on your own, Augusta."

"I should have liked the opportunity to try," Augusta whispered, hardly able to form the words she wanted so desperately to say.

"You had the summer Season," Lady Elmsworth retorted with a shrug. "Do you not recall?"

Augusta closed her eyes. The summer Season had been her first outing into society, and she had enjoyed every moment of it. Her father and mother had made it quite plain that this was not to be the year where she found a husband but rather a time for her to enjoy society, to become used to what it meant to live as a member of the *ton*. The little Season and the summer Season thereafter, she had been told, would be the ones for her to seek out a husband.

And now, that had been pulled away from her before she had even had the opportunity to be amongst the gentlemen of the *beau monde*.

"As I have said," Lady Elmsworth continued, briskly, ignoring Augusta's complaint and the clear expression of shock on her face, "there is no need for you to do anything other than dress in the gown we chose together and then to ensure that you greet Lord Pendleton with all refinement and propriety."

Augusta closed her eyes. "Lord Pendleton?" she repeated, tremulously, already afraid that this gentleman was some older, wealthy gentleman who, for whatever reason, had not been able to find a wife and thus had been more than eager to accept her father's offer.

"Did I not say?" Lady Elmsworth replied, sounding somewhat distracted. She rose quickly, her skirts swishing noisily as she walked towards the door. "He is brother to the Marquess of Leicestershire. A fine gentleman, by all accounts." She shrugged. "He is quiet and perhaps a little dull, but he will do very well for you." One of the maids held the door open, and before Augusta could say more, her mother swept out of the room and the door was closed tightly behind her.

Augusta waited for tears to come but they did not even begin to make their way towards her eyes. She was numb all over, cold and afraid of what was to come. This was not something she had even considered a possibility when it came to her own considerations for what the little Season would hold. There had always been the belief that she would be able to dance, converse, and laugh with as many gentlemen as thought to seek her out. In time, there would be courtships and one gentleman in particular might bring themselves to her notice. There would be excitement and anticipation, nights spent reading and re-reading notes and letters from the gentleman in question, her heart quickening at the thought of marrying him.

But now, such thoughts were gone from her. There was to be none of what she had expected, what she had hoped for. Instead, there was to be a meeting and an arrangement, with no passion or excitement.

Augusta closed her eyes and finally felt a sting of tears. Dropping her head into her hands, she let her emotions roar to life, sending waves of feeling crashing through her until, finally, Augusta wept.

CHAPTER ONE

Quite why he had arranged to be present this evening, Stephen did not know. He ought to have stated that he would meet Lady Augusta in a quieter setting than a ball so that he might have talked with her at length rather than forcing a quick meeting upon them both in a room where it was difficult to hear one's own voice such was the hubbub of the crowd.

He sighed and looked all about him again, finding no delight in being in the midst of society once more. He was a somewhat retiring gentleman, finding no pleasure in the gossip and rumors that flung themselves all around London during the little Season, although it was always much worse during the summer Season. Nor did he appreciate the falseness of those who came to speak and converse with him, knowing full well that the only reason they did so was to enquire after his brother, the Marquess of Leicestershire.

His brother was quite the opposite in both looks and

character, for where Stephen had light brown hair with blue eyes, his brother had almost black hair with dark brown eyes that seemed to pierce into the very soul of whomever he was speaking with. The ladies of the *ton* wanted nothing more than to be in the presence of Lord Leicestershire and, given he was absent from society, they therefore came towards Stephen in order to find out what they could about his brother.

It was all quite wearisome, and Stephen did not enjoy even a moment of it. He was not as important as his brother, he knew, given he did not hold the high title nor have the same amount of wealth as Lord Leicestershire, but surely his own self, his conversation and the like, was of *some* interest? He grinned wryly to himself as he picked up a glass from the tray held by a footman, wondering silently to himself that, if he began to behave as his brother had done on so many occasions, whether or not that would garner him a little more interest from rest of the *ton*.

"You look much too contented," said a familiar voice, and Stephen looked to his left to see his acquaintance, Lord Dryden, approach him. Lord Dryden, a viscount, had an estate near the border to Scotland and, whilst lower in title than Stephen, had become something of a close acquaintance these last two years.

"Lord Dryden," Stephen grinned, slapping the gentleman on the back. "How very good to see you again."

Lord Dryden chuckled. "And you," he said with an honest look in his eyes. "Now, tell me why you are standing here smiling to yourself when I know very well that a ball is not the sort of event you wish to attend?"

Stephen's grin remained on his lips, his eyes alighting on various young ladies that swirled around him. "I was merely considering what my life might be like if I chose to live as my brother does," he answered, with a shrug. "I should have all of society chasing after me, I suppose, although a good many would turn their heads away from me with the shame of being in my company."

"That is quite true," Lord Dryden agreed, no smile on his face but rather a look of concern. "You do not wish to behave so, I hope?"

"No, indeed, I do not," Stephen answered firmly, his smile fading away. "I confess that I am growing weary of so many in the *ton* coming to seek me out simply because they wish to know more about my brother."

"He is not present this evening?"

Stephen snorted. "He is not present for the little Season," he replied with a shrug of his shoulders. "Do not ask me what he has been doing, or why he has such a notable absence, for I fear I cannot tell you." Setting his shoulders, he let out a long breath. "No, I must look to my future."

"Indeed," Lord Dryden responded, an interested look on his face as he eyed Stephen speculatively. "And what is it about your future that you now consider?"

Stephen cleared his throat, wondering whether he ought to tell his friend even though such an arrangement had not yet been completely finalized. "I am to consider myself betrothed very soon," he said before he lost his nerve and kept such news to himself. "I am to meet the lady here this evening. Her father has already signed the papers and they await me in my study." He shrugged one shoulder. "I am sure that, provided she has not lost all of her teeth and that her voice is pleasant enough, the betrothal will go ahead as intended."

Lord Dryden stared at Stephen for a few moments, visible shock rippling over his features. His eyes were wide and his jaw slack, without even a single flicker of mirth in his gaze as he looked back at him. Stephen felt his stomach drop, now worried that Lord Dryden would make some remark that would then force Stephen to reconsider all that he had decided thus far, fearful now that he had made some foolish mistake.

"Good gracious!" Lord Dryden began to laugh, his hand grasping Stephen's shoulder tightly. "You are betrothed?" Shaking his head, he let out another wheezing laugh before straightening and looking Stephen directly in the eye. "I should have expected such a thing from you, I suppose, given you are always entirely practical and very well-considered, but I had not expected it so soon!"

"So soon?" Stephen retorted with a chuckle. "I have been in London for the last three Seasons and have found not even a single young lady to be interested in even conversing with me without needing to talk solely about my brother." His lip curled, a heaviness sitting back on his shoulders as he let out a long sigh. "Therefore, this seemed to be the wisest and the most practical of agreements."

Lord Dryden chuckled again, his eyes still filled with good humor. "I am glad to hear it," he said warmly. "I do congratulate you, of course! Pray, forgive me for my humor. It is only that it has come as something of a surprise to hear such a thing from you yet, now that I consider it, it makes a good deal of sense!" He chuckled again and the sound began to grate on Stephen, making him frown as he returned his friend's sharp look.

Lord Dryden did not appear to care, even if he did notice Stephen's ire. Instead, he leaned a little closer, his eyes bright with curiosity. "Pray, tell me," he began as Stephen nodded, resigning himself to a good many questions. "Who is this lady? Is she of good quality?"

"Very good, yes," Stephen replied, aware, while he did not know the lady's features or character, that she came from a good family line and that breeding would not be a cause for concern. "She is Lady Augusta, daughter to the Earl of Elmsworth."

Lord Dryden's eyes widened, and his smile faded for a moment. "Goodness," he said quietly, looking at Stephen as though he feared his friend had made some sort of dreadful mistake. "And you have met the lady in question?"

"I am to meet her this evening," Stephen answered quickly, wondering why Lord Dryden now appeared so surprised. "I have not heard anything disreputable about her, however." He narrowed his gaze and looked at his friend sharply. "Why? Have you heard some rumor I have not?"

Lord Dryden held up both his hands in a gesture of defense. "No, indeed not!" he exclaimed, sounding quite horrified. "No, tis only that she is a lady who is very well thought of in society. She is well known to everyone, seeks to converse with them all, and has a good many admirers." One shoulder lifted in a half shrug. "To know that her father has sought out an arrangement for her surprises me a little, that is all."

"Because she could do very well without requiring an arrangement," Stephen said slowly understanding what Lord Dryden meant. "Her father appeared to be quite eager to arrange such a thing, however." He sighed and looked all about him, wondering when Lord Elmsworth and his daughter would appear. "He and I spoke at Whites when the matter of his daughter came up."

"And the arrangement came from there?" Lord Dryden asked as Stephen nodded. "I see." He lapsed into silence for a moment, then nodded as though satisfied that he had asked all the questions he wished. "Very good. Then may I be the first to congratulate you!" Lord Dryden's smile returned, and he held out a hand for Stephen to shake. Stephen did so after only a momentary hesitation, reminding himself that there was not, as yet, a complete agreement between himself and Lord Elmsworth.

"I still have to sign and return the papers," he reminded Lord Dryden, who made a noise in the back of his throat before shrugging. "You do not think there will be any difficulty there, I presume?"

"Of course there will not be any difficulty," Lord Dryden retorted with a roll of his eyes. "Lady Augusta is very pleasing, indeed. I am sure you will have no particular difficulty with her."

Stephen opened his mouth to respond, only to see someone begin to approach him. His heart quickened in his chest as he looked at them a little more carefully, seeing Lord Elmsworth approaching and, with him, a young lady wearing a primrose yellow gown. She had an elegant and slender figure and was walking in a most demure fashion, with eyes that lingered somewhere near his knees rather than looking up into people's faces. Her dark brown hair was pulled away from her face, with one or two small ringlets tumbling down near her temples, so as to soften the severity of it. When she dared a glance at him, he was certain he caught a hint of emerald green in her eyes. Almost immediately, her gaze returned to the floor as she dropped into a curtsy, Lord Elmsworth only a step or two in front of her.

"Lord Pendleton!" Lord Elmsworth exclaimed, shaking Stephen's hand with great enthusiasm. "Might I present my daughter, Lady Augusta." He beamed at his daughter, who was only just rising from what had been a perfect curtsy.

"Good evening, Lady Augusta," Stephen said, bowing before her. "I presume your father has already made quite plain who I am?" He looked keenly into her face, and when she lifted her eyes to his, he felt something strike at his heart.

It was not warmth, however, nor a joy that she was quietly beautiful. It did not chime with happiness or contentment but rather with a warning. A warning that Lady Augusta was not as pleased with this arrangement as he. A warning that he might come to trouble if he continued as had been decided. She was looking at him with a hardness in her gaze that hit him hard. There was a coldness, a reserve in her expression, that he could not escape. Clearly, Lady Augusta was not at all contented with the arrangement her father had made for her, which, in turn, did not bode well for him.

"Yes," Lady Augusta said after a moment or two, her voice just as icy as her expression. "Yes, my father has informed of who you are, Lord Pendleton." She looked away, her chin lifted, clearly finding there to be no desire otherwise to say anything more.

Stephen cleared his throat, glancing towards Lord Dryden, who was, to his surprise, not watching Lady Augusta as he had expected, but rather had his attention focused solely on Lord Elmsworth. There was a dark frown on his face; his eyes narrowed just a little and a clear dislike began to ripple across his expression. What was it that Lord Dryden could see that Stephen himself could not?

"Might I introduce Viscount Dryden?" he said quickly, before he could fail in his duties. "Viscount Dryden, this is the Earl of Elmsworth and his daughter—"

"We are already acquainted," Lord Dryden interrupted, bowing low before lifting his head, looking nowhere but at Lady Augusta. "It is very pleasant to see you again, Lady Augusta. I hope you are enjoying the start of the little Season."

Something in her expression softened, and Stephen saw Lady Augusta's mouth curve into a gentle smile. She answered Lord Dryden politely and Stephen soon found himself growing a little embarrassed at the easy flow of conversation between his friend and his betrothed. There was not that ease of manner within himself, he realized, dropping his head just a little so as to regain his sense of composure.

"Perhaps I might excuse myself for a short time," Lord Elmsworth interrupted before Lord Dryden could ask Lady Augusta another question. "Lady Elmsworth is standing but a short distance away and will be watching my daughter closely."

Stephen glanced to his right and saw an older lady looking directly at him, her sense of haughtiness rushing towards him like a gust of wind. There was no contentment in her eyes, but equally, there was no dislike either. Rather, there was the simple expectation that this was how things were to be done and that they ought to continue without delay.

"But of course, Lord Elmsworth," Stephen said quickly, bowing slightly. "I should like to sign your daughter's dance card, if I may?"

"I think," came Lady Augusta's voice, sharp and brittle, "then if that is the case, you ought to be asking the lady herself whether or not she has any space remaining on her card for you to do such a thing, Lord Pendleton."

There came an immediate flush of embarrassment onto Stephen's face, and he cleared his throat whilst Lord Elmsworth sent a hard glance towards his daughter, which she ignored completely. Only Lord Dryden chuckled, the sound breaking the tension and shattering it into a thousand pieces as Stephen looked away.

"You are quite correct to state such a thing, Lady Augusta," Lord Dryden said, easily. "You must forgive my friend. I believe he was a little apprehensive about this meeting and perhaps has forgotten quite how things are done."

Stephen's smile was taut, but he forced it to his lips regardless. "But of course, Lady Augusta," he said tightly. "Might you inform me whether or not you have any spaces on your dance card that I might then be able to take from you?" He bowed his head and waited for her to respond, seeing Lord Elmsworth move away from them all without waiting to see what his daughter would say.

"I thank you for your kind consideration in requesting such a thing from me," Lady Augusta answered, a little too saucily for his liking. "Yes, I believe I do have a few spaces, Lord Pendleton. Please, choose whichever you like." She handed him her dance card and then pulled her hand back, the ribbon sliding from her wrist as he looked down at it. She turned her head away as if she did not want to see where he wrote his name, and this, in itself, sent a flurry of anger down Stephen's spine. What was wrong with this young lady? Was she not glad that she was now betrothed, that she would soon have a husband and become mistress of his estate?

For a moment, he wondered if he had made a mistake in agreeing to this betrothal, feeling a swell of relief in his chest that he had not yet signed the agreement, only for Lord Dryden to give him a tiny nudge, making him realize he had not yet written his name down on the dance card but was, in fact, simply staring at it as though it might provide him with all the answers he required.

"The country dance, mayhap," he said, a little more loudly than he had intended. "Would that satisfy you, Lady Augusta?"

She turned her head and gave him a cool look, no smile gracing her lips. "But of course," she said with more sweetness than he had expected. "I would be glad to dance with you, Lord Pendleton. The country dance sounds quite wonderful."

He frowned, holding her gaze for a moment longer before dropping his eyes back to her dance card again and writing his name there. Handing it back to her, he waited for her to smile, to acknowledge what he had given her, only for her to sniff, bob a curtsy and turn away. Stephen's jaw worked furiously, but he remained standing steadfastly watching after her, refusing to allow himself to chase after her and demand to know what she meant by such behavior. Instead, he kept his head lifted and his eyes fixed, thinking to himself that he had, most likely, made a mistake.

"I would ascertain from her behavior that this betrothal has come as something of a shock," Lord Dryden murmured, coming closer to Stephen and looking after Lady Augusta with interest. "She was less than pleased to be introduced to you, that is for certain!"

Stephen blew out his frustration in a long breath, turning his eyes away from Lady Augusta and looking at his friend. "I think I have made a mistake," he said gruffly. "That young lady will not do at all! She is—"

"She is overcome," Lord Dryden interrupted, holding up one hand to stem the protest from Stephen's lips. "As I have said, I think this has been something of a shock to her. You may recall that I said I am acquainted with Lady Augusta already and I know that how she presented herself this evening is not her usual character."

Stephen shook his head, his lips twisting as he considered what he was to do. "I am not certain that I have made the wisest decision," he said softly. "Obviously, I require a wife and that does mean that I shall have to select someone from amongst the *ton,* but—"

"Lady Augusta is quite suitable," Lord Dryden interrupted firmly. "And, if you were quite honest with yourself, Lord Pendleton, I think you would find that such an arrangement suits you very well. After all—" He gestured to the other guests around him. "You are not at all inclined to go out amongst the *ton* and find a lady of your choosing, are you?"

Stephen sighed heavily and shot Lord Dryden a wry look. "That is true enough, I suppose."

"Then trust me when I say that Lady Augusta is more than suitable for you," Lord Dryden said again, with such fervor that Stephen felt as though he had no other choice to believe him. "Sign the betrothal agreement and know that Lady Augusta will not be as cold towards you in your marriage as she has been this evening." He chuckled and slapped Stephen on the shoulder. "May I be the first to offer you my congratulations."

Smiling a little wryly, Stephen found himself nodding. "Very well," he told Lord Dryden. "I accept your congratulations with every intention of signing the betrothal agreement when I return home this evening."

"Capital!" Lord Dryden boomed, looking quite satisfied with himself. "Then I look forward to attending your wedding in the knowledge that it was I who brought it about." He chuckled and then, spotting a young lady coming towards him quickly excused himself. Stephen smiled as he saw Lord Dryden offer his arm to the young lady and then step out on to the floor. His friend was correct. Lady Augusta was, perhaps, a little overwhelmed with all that had occurred and simply was not yet open to the fact that she would soon be his wife. In time, she would come to be quite happy with him and their life together; he was sure of it. He had to thrust his worries aside and accept his decisions for what they were.

"I shall sign it the moment I return home," he said aloud to himself as though confirming this was precisely what he intended to do. With a small sigh of relief at his decision, he lifted his chin and set his shoulders. Within the week, everyone would know of his betrothal to Lady Augusta and that, he decided, brought him a good deal of satisfaction.

His quill hovered over the line for just a moment but, with a clenching of his jaw, Stephen signed his name on the agreement. His breath shot out of him with great fury, leaving him swallowing hard, realizing what he had done. It was now finalized. He would marry Lady Augusta, and the banns would have to be called very soon, given her father wanted her wed before the end of the little Season. Letting out his breath slowly, he rolled up the papers and began to prepare his seal, only for there to come a hurried knock at the door. He did not even manage to call out for his servant to enter, for the butler rushed in before he could open his mouth.

"Do forgive me, my lord," the butler exclaimed, breathing hard from his clear eagerness to reach Stephen in time. "This came from your brother's estate with a most urgent request that you read it at once."

Startled, his stomach twisting one way and then the other, Stephen took the note from the butler's hand and opened it, noting that there was no print on the seal. His heart began to pound as he read the news held within.

"My brother is dead," he whispered, one hand gripping onto the edge of his desk for support. "He...he was shot in a duel and died on the field." Closing his eyes, Stephen let the news wash over him, feeling all manner of strong emotions as he fought to understand what had occurred. His brother had passed away, then, lost to the grave, and out of nothing more than his foolishness. To have been fighting in a duel meant that Leicestershire had done something of the most grievous nature—whether it had been stealing another man's wife or taking affections from some unfortunate young lady without any intention of pursuing the matter further.

Running one hand over his face, Stephen felt the weight of his grief come to settle on his heart, his whole body seeming to ache with a pain he had only experienced once before when their dear father had passed away. His throat constricted as he thought of his mother. He would have to go to her at once, to comfort her in the midst of her sorrow. Yes, his brother had packed her off to the Dower House long before she was due to reside there, and yes, there had been some difficulties between them, but Stephen knew that she had loved her eldest son and would mourn the loss of him greatly.

A groan came from his lips as he lifted his head and tried to focus on his butler. His vision was blurry, his head feeling heavy and painful.

"Ready my carriage at once," he rasped, "and have my things sent after me. I must return to my brother's estate."

The butler bowed. "At once," he said, his concern clear in his wide-eyed expression. "I beg your pardon for my intrusion, my lord, but is Lord Leicestershire quite well?"

Stephen looked at his faithful butler, knowing that the man had worked for the family for many years in keeping the townhouse in London readied for them and understood that his concern was genuine. "My brother is dead," he said hoarsely as the butler gasped in horror. "I have lost him. He is gone, and I shall never see him again."

CHAPTER TWO

S*ix months later*

Augusta rolled her eyes as her mother brought out the primrose yellow dress that she had worn at the start of the little Season some six months ago. She sighed as her mother spread it out with one hand, a look in her eye that told Augusta she was not about to escape this easily.

"That gown was for the winter, Mama," she said, calmly. "I cannot wear it again now that the sun is shining and the air is so very warm." She gestured to it with a look of what she hoped was sadness on her face. "Besides, it is not quite up to the fashion for this current Season."

Her mother tutted. "Nonsense, Augusta," she said briskly. "There is very little need for you to purchase new gowns when you are to have a trousseau. Your betrothed has, as you know, recently lost his brother and as such, will need to find some happiness in all that he does. I must hope that your presence will bring him a little joy in his sorrow and, in wearing the very same gown as you were first introduced to him in, I am certain that Lord Pendleton—I mean, Lord Leicestershire—will be very happy to see you again."

Augusta said nothing, silently disagreeing with her mother and having no desire whatsoever to greet her betrothed again, whether in her primrose yellow gown or another gown entirely. She had felt compassion and sympathy for his loss, yes, but she had silently reveled in her newfound freedom. Indeed, given their betrothal had not yet been confirmed and given the *ton* knew nothing of it, Augusta had spent the rest of the little Season enjoying herself, silently ignoring the knowledge that within the next few months, she would have to let everyone in the *ton* know of her engagement.

But not yet, it seemed. She had spoken to her father, and he had confirmed that the papers had not been returned by Lord Leicestershire but had urged her not to lose hope, stating that he had every reason to expect the gentleman to do just as he had promised but that he was permitting him to have some time to work through his grief before pressing him about the arrangement.

And when news had been brought that the new Marquess of Leicestershire had come to London for the Season, her father had taken it as confirmation that all was just as it ought to be. He was quite contented with the situation as things stood, silently certain that when Lord Leicestershire was ready, he would approach the Earl himself or speak directly to Augusta.

"I will not wear that gown, Mama," Augusta said frostily. "I am well aware of what you hope for but I cannot agree. That gown is not at all suitable for Lord Stonington's ball! I must find something that is quite beautiful, Mama." She saw her mother frown and tried quickly to come up with some reason for her to agree to such a change. "I know your intentions are good," she continued, swiftly, "but Lord Leicestershire will be glad to see me again no matter what I am wearing; I am sure of it. And, Mama, if I wear the primrose yellow gown, might it not remind him of the night that he was told of his brother's death?" She let her voice drop low, her eyes lowering dramatically. "The night when he had no other choice but to run from London so that he might comfort his mother and tidy up the ruin his brother left behind."

"Augusta!" Lady Elmsworth's voice was sharp. "Do not speak in such a callous manner!"

Augusta, who was nothing if not practical, looked at her mother askance. "I do not consider speaking the truth plainly to be callous, Mama," she said quite calmly. "After all, it is not as though Lord Leicestershire's brother was anything other than a scoundrel." She shrugged, turning away from her mother and ignoring the horrified look on her face. "Everyone in London is well aware what occurred."

She herself had been unable to escape the gossip and, to her shame, had listened to it eagerly at times. The late Lord Leicestershire had lost his life in a duel that had not gone well for him. He had taken a young lady of quality and attempted to steal kisses—and perhaps more—from her, only to be discovered by the young lady's brother, who was a viscount of some description. Despite the fact that such duels were frowned upon, one had taken place and the gentleman who had done such a dreadful thing to a young lady of society had paid the ultimate price for his actions. A part of her did feel very sorry indeed for the newly titled Lord Leicestershire, knowing that he must have had to endure a good deal of struggle, difficulty and pain in realizing not only what his brother had done but in taking on all the responsibilities that now came with his new title.

"I should think you better than to listen to gossip," Lady Elmsworth said, primly. "Now, Augusta, do stop being difficult and wear what I ask of you."

"No," Augusta replied quite firmly, surprising both herself and her mother with her vehemence. "No, I shall not." Taking in the look of astonishment on her mother's face, Augusta felt her spirits lift very high indeed as she realized that, if she spoke with determination, her mother might, in fact, allow her to do as she wished. She had, thus far, always bowed to her mother's authority, but ever since she had discovered that her marriage was already planned for her and that she was to have no independence whatsoever, she had found a small spark growing steadily within her. A spark that determined that she find some way to have a little autonomy, even if it would only be for a short time.

"I will wear the light green silk," she said decisively, walking to her wardrobe and indicating which one she meant. "It brings out my complexion a little more, I think." She smiled to herself and touched the fabric gently. "And I believe it brings a little more attention to my eyes."

Lady Elmsworth sighed heavily but, thankfully, she set down the primrose yellow and then proceeded to seat herself in a chair by the fire, which was not lit today given the warmth of the afternoon. "You think this is the most suitable choice, then?"

"I do," Augusta said firmly. "I shall wear this and have a few pearls and perhaps a ribbon set into my hair." Again, she smiled but did not see her mother's dark frown. "And perhaps that beautiful diamond pendant around my neck."

Lady Elmsworth's frown deepened. "You need not try to draw attention to yourself, Augusta," she reminded her sternly. "You are betrothed. You will be wed to Lord Leicestershire and he is the only one you need attempt to impress."

Augusta hid the sigh from her mother as she turned back to her wardrobe, closing the door carefully so as not to crush any of her gowns. A part of her hoped that she would not have to marry Lord Leicestershire, for given he had not yet returned the betrothal agreement to her father, there seemed to be no eagerness on his part to do so or to proceed with their engagement. Mayhap, now that he was of a great and high title, he might find himself a little more interested in the young ladies of the *ton* and would not feel the need to sign the betrothal agreement at all. It might all come to a very satisfactory close, and she could have the freedom she had always expected.

"Augusta!" Lady Elmsworth's voice was sharp, as though she knew precisely what it was Augusta was thinking. "You will make sure that all of your attention is on your betrothed this evening. Do you understand me?"

"We are not betrothed yet, Mama," Augusta replied a little tartly. "Therefore, I cannot show him any specific attention for fear of what others might say." She arched one eyebrow and looked at her mother as she turned around, aware she was irritating her parent but finding a dull sense of satisfaction in her chest. "Once the agreement has been sent to Papa, then, of course, I shall do my duty." She dropped into a quick curtsy, her eyes low and her expression demure, but it did not fool Lady Elmsworth.

"You had best be very careful with your behavior this evening, Augusta," she exclaimed, practically throwing herself from her chair as she rose to her feet, her cheeks a little pink and her eyes blazing with an unexpressed frustration. "I shall be watching you most carefully."

"Of course, Mama," Augusta replied quietly, permitting herself a small smile as her mother left the room, clearly more than a little irritated with all that Augusta had said. Augusta let a long breath escape her, feeling a sense of anticipation and anxiety swirl all about within her as she considered what was to come this evening. Lord Leicestershire would be present, she knew, for whilst he had not written to her directly to say such a thing, all of London was abuzz with the news that the new Marquess had sent his acceptance to Lord Stonington's ball. Everyone would want to look at him, to see his face and to wonder just how like his brother he might prove to be. Everyone, of course, except for Augusta. She would greet him politely, of course, but had no intention of showing any interest in him whatsoever. Perhaps that, combined with his new title and his new appreciation from the *ton,* might decide that she was no longer a suitable choice for a wife.

Augusta could only hope.

"GOOD EVENING, LADY AUGUSTA."

Augusta gasped in surprise as she turned to see who had spoken her name, before throwing herself into the arms of a lovely lady. "Lady Mary!" she cried, delighted to see her dear friend again. They had shared one Season already as debutantes and had become very dear friends indeed, and Augusta had missed her at the little Season. "How very glad I am to see you again. I am in desperate need of company and you have presented yourself to me at the very moment that I need you!"

Lady Mary laughed and squeezed Augusta's hand. "But of course," she said, a twinkle in her eye. "I knew very well that you would need a dear friend to walk through this Season with you—just as I need one also!" She turned and looked at the room, the swirling colors of the gowns moving all around them, and let out a contented sigh. "I am quite certain that this Season, we shall both find a suitable match, and I, for one, am eagerly looking forward to the courtship, the excitement and the wonderfulness that is sure to follow!"

Augusta could not join in with the delight that Lady Mary expressed, her heart suddenly heavy and weighted as it dropped in her chest. Lady Mary noticed at once, her joyous smile fading as she looked into Augusta's face.

"My dear friend, whatever is the matter?"

Augusta opened her mouth to answer, only for her gaze to snag on something. Or, rather, a familiar face that seemed to loom out of the crowd towards her, her heart slamming hard as she realized who it was.

"Lady Augusta?"

Lady Mary's voice seemed to be coming from very far away as Augusta's eyes fixed upon Lord Leicestershire, her throat constricting and a sudden pain stabbing into her chest. He was standing a short distance away, and even though there were other guests coming in and out of her vision, blocking her view of him entirely upon occasion, she seemed to be able to see him quite clearly. His eyes were fixed to hers, appearing narrowed and dark and filled with nothing akin to either gladness or relief upon seeing her. Her stomach dropped to the floor for an inexplicable reason, making her wonder if he felt the same about her as she did about him. Why did that trouble her, she wondered, unable to tug her gaze from his. She should be able to turn her head away from him at once, should be able to show the same disregard as she had done at their first meeting, should be able to express her same dislike for their arrangement as she had done at the first—but for whatever reason, she was not able to do it.

"Lady Augusta, you are troubling me now!"

Lady Mary's voice slowly came back to her ears, growing steadily louder until the hubbub of the room appeared to be much louder than before. She closed her eyes tightly, finally freed from Lord Leicestershire's gaze, and felt her whole body tremble with a strange shudder.

"Lady Mary," she breathed, her hand touching her friend's arm. "I—I apologize. It is only that I have seen my betrothed and I—"

"Your betrothed?"

Lady Mary's eyes widened, her cheeks rapidly losing their color as she stared at Augusta with evident concern.

"You are engaged?" Lady Mary whispered as Augusta's throat tightened all the more. "When did such a thing occur?"

Augusta shook her head minutely. "It was not something of my choosing," she answered hoarsely. "My father arranged it on my behalf, without my knowledge of it. When I was present in the little Season, I was introduced to Lord Pendleton."

"Lord Pendleton?" Lady Mary exclaimed, only to close her eyes in embarrassment and drop her head.

Augusta smiled tightly. "Indeed," she said, seeing her friend's reaction and fully expecting her to be aware of the situation regarding Lord Pendleton. "He has not signed the betrothal agreement as far as I am aware, for it has not yet been returned to my father. However, given he has been in mourning for his brother, my father has not been overly eager in pursuing the matter, believing that Lord Leicestershire—as he is now—will return the papers when he is quite ready."

Lady Mary said nothing for some moments, considering all that had been said carefully and letting her eyes rove towards where Augusta had been looking towards only a few moments before.

"That is most extraordinary," she said, one hand now pressed against her heart. "And might I inquire as to whether or not you are pleased with this arrangement?"

With a wry smile, Augusta said nothing but looked at her friend with a slight lift of her eyebrow, making Lady Mary more than aware of precisely how she felt.

"I see," Lady Mary replied, her eyes still wide but seeming to fill with sympathy as she squeezed Augusta's hand, her lips thin. "I am sorry that you have had to endure such difficulties. I cannot imagine what you must have felt to be told that your marriage was all arranged without you having any awareness of such a thing beforehand!"

"It has been rather trying," Augusta admitted softly. "I have a slight hope through it all, however."

"Oh?"

Allowing herself another smile, Augusta dared a glance back towards Lord Leicestershire, only to see him still watching her. Embarrassed, she pulled her eyes away quickly, looking back to her friend. "I have a slight hope that he might decide *not* to sign the papers," she said as Lady Mary sucked in a breath. "As he is now a marquess and an heir, what if he decides that he must now choose his bride with a good deal more consideration?" Feeling a little more relaxed, no longer as anxious and as confused as she had been only a few moments before, she allowed herself a small smile. "I might be able to discover my freedom once more."

Lady Mary did not smile. Rather, her lips twisted to one side, and her brows lowered. "But would that not then mean that your father might, once again, find you another match of his choosing?" she said quietly, as though she were afraid to upset Augusta any further. "Lord Leicestershire is certainly an excellent match, Lady Augusta. He is a marquess and will have an excellent fortune. Surely he is not to be dismissed with such ease!"

Augusta allowed herself to frown, having not considered such a thing before. She did not want to be saddled with anyone of her father's choosing, instead wanting to discover a husband of her own choice. There was that choice there that, up until the previous little Season, she had always expected to have.

"I will simply speak to my father," she said airily, trying to express some sort of expectation that her father would do precisely what she asked. "He will be willing to listen to me, I am sure."

Lady Mary's expression cleared. "Well, if that is true, then I must hope that you can extricate yourself from this...if you so wish." That flickering frown remained, reminding Augusta that she was now betrothed to a marquess. A Marquess who had influence, wealth, and a high title. Was she being foolish hoping that the betrothal would come to an end? Did she truly value her own choice so much that she would throw aside something that so many others in society would pursue with everything they had?

"I..." Augusta trailed off, looking into her friend's eyes and knowing that, with Lady Mary, she had to be honest.

"I shall consider what you have said," she agreed eventually as Lady Mary's frown finally lifted completely. "You are right to state that he *is*, in fact, a marquess, and mayhap he is not a match that I should be so eager to thrust aside."

"Might I inquire as to how often you have been in his company?" Lady Mary asked, turning to stand beside Augusta so that she might look out through the ballroom a little better. "Do you know him *very* well? Does he have a difficult personality that makes your eagerness to wed him so displeasing?"

Augusta winced as a knowing look came into Lady Mary's eyes. "I confess that I have not spent any time with him at all," she admitted, "save for our introduction and, thereafter, a country dance." She lifted one shoulder in a half shrug whilst avoiding Lady Mary's gaze. "Perhaps I have been a little hasty."

Lady Mary chuckled and nodded. "Mayhap," she agreed, with a smile that lit up her expression. "He may very well be a very fine gentleman indeed, Lady Augusta, and soon, you will be considered the most fortunate of all the young ladies present in London for the Season."

As much as Augusta did not want to accept this, as much as she wanted to remain determined to make her own choice, she had to admit that Lady Mary had made some valid considerations and she ought to take some time to think through all that had been said. It was not with trepidation but with a sense of curiosity deep within her that she walked through the ballroom with Lady Mary by her side, ready to greet Lord Leicestershire again. There was a little more interest in her heart and mind now, wondering what he would say and how he would appear when he greeted her. With a deep breath, she smiled brightly as she drew near him, her heart quickening just a little as she curtsied.

"Lord Leicestershire," she said, lifting her eyes to his and noting, with a touch of alarm, that there was not even a flicker of a smile touching his lips. "Good evening. How very good to see you again."

Lord Leicestershire frowned, his brow furrowed and his eyes shadowed. "Pardon me, my lady," he said as the other gentlemen he was talking to turned their attention towards both her and Lady Mary. "But I do not recall your name. In fact," he continued, spreading his hands, "I do not think we have ever been acquainted!"

Augusta's mouth dropped open in astonishment, her eyes flaring wide and her cheeks hot with embarrassment as she saw each of the gentlemen looking at her and then glancing at each other with amusement. Lady Mary gaped at Lord Leicestershire, her hand now on Augusta's elbow.

"If you will excuse me," Augusta croaked, trying to speak with strength only for her to practically whisper. "I must..."

"You are due to dance," Lady Mary interjected, helpfully guiding Augusta away from Lord Leicestershire. "Come, Lady Augusta."

Augusta let her friend lead her from the group, feeling utter humiliation wash all over her. Keeping her head low, she allowed Lady Mary to guide her to the opposite side of the room, silently praying that no one else was watching her. Glancing from one side to the other, she heard the whispers and laughter coming from either side of her and closed her eyes tightly, fearful that the rumors and gossip were already starting. For whatever reason, Lord Leicestershire had either chosen to pretend he did not know her or truly had forgotten her, and either way, Augusta was completely humiliated.

WHAT HAPPENS next with Lady Augusta and Lord Leicestershire? Will they continue to fight or will they find a way to respect each other? Check out the rest of the story in the Kindle Store A Broken Betrothal

JOIN MY MAILING LIST

Sign up for my newsletter to stay up to date on new releases, contests, giveaways, freebies, and deals!

Free book with signup!

Monthly Giveaways! Books and Amazon gift cards!
Join me on Facebook: https://www.
facebook.com/rosepearsonauthor

Website: www.RosePearsonAuthor.com

Follow me on Goodreads: Author Page

You can also follow me on Bookbub!
Click on the picture below – see the Follow button?

Made in the USA
Middletown, DE
15 March 2021